Three Wishes

Heart of the Djinn
Book One

Lisa Manifold

ISBN: 1-943530-041
ISBN-13: 978-1-943530-04-5

DEDICATION

To My Darling Boys:
Always, always take the chance!

Love you !

Mom

ACKNOWLEDGMENTS

No book is ever done on an island. Mine are no different.
My critique groups—Monica, Shawn, Deb, Lynne, Julie,
Craig, Cordia, Janet, and Joel— are amazing. You keep me
sane and grounded. My editor, the fabulous Rachel Millar,
makes sure that I don't write 80's cliché. For which I am
eternally grateful. Although as a child of the 80's, I kind of
like the cliché. Any leftover mistakes, are, of course, all my
doing. She does her best, honestly! To Corinne and Wendy
for helping me to stay focused, and for being the ears I
needed to bend. To Jen, Tara, and Pam—for being an ear
for everything else not writing related. To my family—
Mom, Dad, Dick, Liz, Shannon, and Mike—the best damn
cheerleaders anyone could have.
To Ms. Lynn E, for helping to hold down things on a
front that I worried about obsessively. We know now it
wasn't a worry at all, but I appreciate you being there to
help carry the load. That help allowed me to work.
To my Darling Boys, to whom this work is dedicated.
Finally, to my wonderful husband Jimmy. Your support
carries me through when I have doubts.

I love you all, and count myself fortunate to have all of
you in my life.

Three Wishes

Lisa Manifold

CHAPTER ONE

Present Day
Tibby

I walked into the conference room. This would be a piece of cake. The dispute wasn't that big of a deal, though our client was making one out of it. Like all Granddad's friends, everything was a big deal. Probably why they were all, to a man, filthy rich. Maybe I needed to get that mindset.

I laughed inwardly and shrugged the thought away. I'd go insane. Kind of like most of Granddad's friends. I liked my life, my practice, and the way things in my life were going. I put my general state of satisfaction aside and focused on the meeting at hand.

"Mr. Barrington?" I held out my hand to the older gentleman in the room. He stood with two younger men, and he turned when I said his name.

"I'm Tabitha Holloway and this is my partner, Bryant Higgs. We represent—"

"Tibby?"

Two different voices called me by my nickname. Both held tones of shock and surprise. I opened my mouth to respond when I looked, really looked at who was talking to me.

Oh my god. I felt faint suddenly when I realized who they were.

Just as suddenly, I looked around for the telltale flash of glitter. I was going to end up back in my room three years earlier. I could feel it.

Back to when I was…well, for lack of a better word, a complete dumb ass. Not the competent, honest, take-charge person I'd become. Shit. Shit, shit, shit. I didn't want to go back there, to that Tibby, away from the life I'd built for myself, piece by piece.

But if this wasn't a crossroad, I didn't know what was.

It had been so long, I honestly thought Dhameer had forgotten me. Because I'd made such a success of myself, and applied what I'd learned, courtesy of the Dhameer School of Second Chances. Back to where this began.

CHAPTER TWO

Three Years Earlier
Tibby

What if? Lately, that seemed the story of my life. Since I worked at home as a website designer, I had plenty of time for self-reflection.

I was lucky. I know that. I had a lot of opportunities, and I let them get away. So now I chose to work at home and stay out of the messy office crap. That office crap was what screwed me up, every time. Get to know people, start being social, and then Bam! I screw it up. Sleep with someone's ex without knowing it. Flirt with the wrong guy, piss off his wife. I'm not a bad person. I know that, deep down. But I make really, really shitty choices. If it weren't for my friend Xavier, I'd be living in a box with all my stuff in a shopping cart. As I was pulling myself out of the mess I'd made of law school, Xavier's star was on the rise. He knew I was good with the IT side of things, and he hired me as his web person. Because of him, I'll always have a job. A career of sorts, because he's brought business my way. I also look over his books to make sure his accountant and financial people aren't screwing him over.

7

Coming from where we grew up, you want someone double checking. Someone at your back. I do that for X. Just like he does for me.

The phone rang. It was Xavier.

"Hey."

"Girl, what's up?"

"Nothing. You're still filthy rich, and people are still honest or scared." Our typical greeting.

He laughed. "I love you, Tib. When are you gonna come live with me and marry me?"

Now it was my turn to laugh. "Never. You're a dog on a good day, X. I love you too, but from afar." We both knew that things could have gone differently, but in the end, we both needed a friend more than anything else. I treasure him like I treasure no one else. I'd never screw that up. At least I have some principles, in spite of what's been said about me over the years.

Talk turned to some updates he wanted, and I took notes. While X has a devil-may-care rep, or more bluntly, a fuck-off rep, he's an amazing businessman. He knows every aspect of his brand. To the world, he's XTC, famous rapper and bad boy. To me, he's smart as hell and my one friend.

"X?"

"Yeah?"

"You ever have regrets?"

I could hear him shifting through the phone. "Regrets for what, Tib?"

"I don't know. Things you didn't take a chance on."

"I took a chance on the things that were important."

"I know that. I mean, like people, or lost

connections, or things you didn't realize were opportunities at the time?"

"Sure. But fuck it. You can't live in regrets. If I did, Marcia would have it all."

We both laughed. Marcia was his latest ex. He'd actually married her, rather than dating her until she got mad and tired of waiting on him and dumped him. I didn't understand why she had been different from all the other exes, but who was I to criticize? I'd been the best man—well, the best woman at their wedding. I loved wearing a tux. All the bridesmaids had glared. Probably because I'd been far more comfortable than they were. I'm sure it had nothing to do with the fact that Marcia hated me on sight. I could understand. A chick as the best friend of a bad-ass rapper? I would have been suspicious too. Maybe not as much of a bitch as she'd been, however.

"You get that all straightened out with her?"

"I don't pay a shark for nothing."

"Good." I left it be. I wasn't one to throw stones in the relationship department.

We chatted for a few more minutes, and then he hung up.

I sighed. I knew he wanted me to live closer, to be more available, but I couldn't. The world he lived in would have fucked me up even more than I was. But I missed him. We'd been friends since elementary school; we both had crappy parents, both had nights of hiding from drunken rages. It bonds you. Thankfully, we'd kept those bonds.

And because of X, I wasn't living in a box with a shopping cart. I set up for the work he wanted done tomorrow and went into the kitchen to make something.

Nothing looked good. I could feel one of those nights coming on. I pulled out the tub of ice cream and parked in front of the TV. Maybe the sugar would calm all this shit down. I hadn't been this unsettled in ages.

After too much ice cream and probably too much Lifetime, I gave up and went to bed. I felt fat and weepy. Not a successful dispelling of whatever this was. Lying in bed, staring at the ceiling, my mind went back to my torturous game of what if. Tonight, for some unknown reason, I wandered into the dreaded I could have moments.

I fell asleep thinking about a couple of those, and about what would have happened had I taken the chance. I did my best to dispel my whiny thoughts from earlier, because I noticed when I went to bed in a bad mood, I had crappy dreams.

When I woke up, the sun was shining through the top of my window. I peered at the clock and saw that it was 6:37. Why hadn't my alarm gone off? It was usually set for 6:30. I must not have set it last night. Oh well. I could afford to sleep in this morning. I began to snuggle back into sleep when something caught my eye. I looked again. There was a man, sitting on the edge of my bed, legs crossed, examining his fingernails. He looked…glittery, a mix of what looked like gold and silver.

"Who the fuck are you?" I screamed, clutching the blanket to my throat with one hand while reaching out for my phone on the night table with the other. It wasn't there. Where the hell had I left it? I tried to look around the room without looking like I was looking around the room. Fuck.

"You can call me your fairy godmother,

Toots," he said cheerfully. Great. A serial killer who was chipper, cheerful, and possessed of a sense of humor. I had to find a way to get to my phone. I cursed myself for not keeping one by the bed.

"Why?"

"Because I heard you last night, and I'm here to help you."

"What? What are you talking about?"

"I heard your dreams. Everyone in the state could. I didn't realize just how loud dreams could sound until I ran across you. So I am here to put to rest your eternal pondering."

"How are you going to do that?" This was creepy, and interesting, and creepy all at once. I figured I could get to the phone in a minute. He was obviously crazy. I was kind of afraid to move.

"I am a djinn." He looked at me as though that explained it all.

I clutched my blanket higher around my neck and cast my eyes around for my phone.

He saw me do it, and sighed heavily. "You may know me as a genie."

"Like Aladdin?" I couldn't help asking, lowering the blanket a little.

He rolled his eyes like the bitchiest girl in high school. "Djinn. In the understood tradition of djinn, I am going to give you three wishes. You must know," he held up an index finger, and I was caught watching it sparkle in the sun. "My wish granting is a little different though. There is no wishing for more wishes. Your wishes are going to have to be specific, and they are going to be what you would call a 'do-over'."

"I'm not trying to be dense here, but what do

you mean?" My curiosity was getting the better of my fear. Everything in the room seemed more in focus, sharper. I knew I ought to be more afraid, but it didn't seem to be happening that way.

He sighed, and rolled his eyes dramatically. Again. Whatever the hell he was, he did not lack in the dramatic flair department. "Humans. I liked you better when you were more savage in your wants as you were in your dreams. Far more willing to believe without question; able to just wish and get it over with. Okay. I'll break it down for you, Tootsie Pop. You have been dreaming of turning points in your life. Those maddening little what ifs. What if you had made choice A instead of choice B? That sort of thing. I am going to grant you three do-overs. You get to choose three times in your life where you wish you had made a different decision, and go back and make the decision you didn't make the first time around. I'll let you see what happens. You and I will talk after you have done all three, and see what's next. What do you say? Are you interested?"

"I don't want to sound ungrateful, but how do I know that you are not just crazy for glitter paint and breaking into houses?" I had decided that if he was crazy, it was better to humor him until I could find my damn phone.

He rolled his eyes again, muttering what sounded like "humans" under his breath. He rose from the bed. When I say rose, he actually lifted off the bed. He didn't seem to have feet. It looked a little misty from the knee area down. He raised a hand, and I saw it shimmer in the sun. He made a gesture that looked like he was throwing something, and suddenly there was a giraffe at the foot of my bed.

CHAPTER THREE

The giraffe looked as shocked as I was. I must have been able to hold it together better than I thought, because unlike the giraffe, I didn't lose bladder control immediately. How do you clean up giraffe pee? How did that thing even fit in my little apartment bedroom? I didn't have time to think about it further because the giraffe changed into a peacock, which screeched at me and shook his feathers. Then the peacock changed into a dragon.

I couldn't believe it. There was a fucking dragon in my room, which, in truth, looked as happy about this as I was. As all disgruntled dragons are wont to do, he roared. With his roaring came flame, and it was aimed right at me.

I shut my eyes and screamed. When I didn't burst into flame, I opened them, and the man? Genie? Was sitting on the edge of the bed again, looking rather smug.

"All right. You're not the average B&E guy. So why me? Why offer me this?"

"As I said, Toots, I heard you. Your dreams were screaming out louder than if you'd been shouting them from the rooftops last night. I'm a sucker for humans. What can I say?"

"What's the catch?"

He laughed then, and it sounded genuine. "Smart girl, aren't you? You know nothing is free. There is really no big catch, although that may not be your perception. I'm a djinn. My purpose in life is to grant wishes. I've been doing this long enough that I'm not beholden to anyone; a free agent, if you will. Even without someone calling the shots for me, it's still who I am, the grantor of wishes. Only now, I can choose whom I wish to offer that to, what kind of terms, that sort of thing. I've gotten picky. I like you. You're a hard worker. Everyone makes some poor choices. You've made some doozies. You don't whine about it, you own your mess and carry on. You don't see that as often as you might think. When I heard your dreams last night, I decided it was time to offer you a second chance."

"Really, you are going to have to work with me here. Can we back up? There are really genies in the world? It's not just a Disney movie?"

"Toots, most things are really in the world. Legends come from somewhere, you know. They don't just sprout, fully formed, from the addled brain of some guy who accidently put the wrong mushroom in his breakfast stew. The world is not as friendly to the legends as it once was. So the stuff of legends stays hidden, out of sight. Humans don't really need magic and amazing miracles like they once did. Well." he tapped his lip, "actually, they probably do, but the technology that's been created has taken the place of magic and miracles and all that. It's not so great for legends still skulking about, but what can you do? I like it, myself. I can still do what I was made to do, and choose those I wish to help. Choice is a wonderful thing when you have gone through so much of your existence without it."

"I can understand that," I said.

"I doubt it, Toots. You've always had choice; you've just made choices you regret. It was always your decision. There was never anyone else making it for you."

"It doesn't feel that way." I felt a little stung.

"That's only because you've never really lost your ability to choose. And now you're getting a chance that most people never have. The chance to live your life while being able to make truly informed choices.

"All right," I said. "Can we go back to the catch? I know there's one."

"Right you are. The catch. I don't see it as much, but you might. Here it is. When you go back, you'll be at the crossroads. I mean, the exact moment where you made a choice that changed your direction, your destiny. You will make your choice, and I hope it's different from the one you lament now, if only to put your musings to rest. All the while, as you are going forward with the consequences of your choice, you will be the you that you are now, on the inside. From the outside, you'll look like the you that you were then, at the time of the crossroads. You'll also need to know that this is not permanent. What happens after you have made a new choice, no one knows. I can't tell. It's all up to you. So I have to warn you, it's not permanent. It could be, but I can't make a call about that at this point."

I leaned back a little, head whirling. This was a lot to take in all at once. If he hadn't trotted the menagerie out in front of me, I would be a lot more skeptical. With that, and the whole issue of his glittery look, and the floating, I had to think that maybe he was for real. An honest to god real mythical creature who was at the moment shedding glitter on my comforter. The idea made me smile.

"So that's it? I get to go back, do over something of my choosing, all while knowing all that I do now? That really doesn't sound like a catch."

He smiled. "I agree, but other humans have come to disagree. It seems the solution to all your problems, so to speak, but when you get what you wish for, it's not always what you really want. Besides, you won't make the decision about where you end up. Big enough of a catch for you?"

"Well, let me see. I work from home fifty hours a week, maybe more. I don't have a lot of friends, mostly because I was stupid, partied too much, and took nothing seriously. I don't date, because I just can't seem to get past the small talk. I honestly wonder if I even like people anymore."

"You're sounding rather embittered, Tootsie pop."

"I may be. I'm living a small life, trying to just be a good person and basically keep to myself. I miss part of who I was. Not the stupid part," I said with a grimace, which made him laugh again, "but the part that loved every bit of life. I feel like life has taken that from me. That hurts because I did work pretty hard to get where I was."

"No one takes anything that you don't willingly give."

"That may be, but it doesn't change the way I feel. I'll take your offer. I want to see what could have happened if I made some different choices in life."

"You are sure? Even knowing that if things turn out peaches and cream, you probably won't get to stay there? The sure knowledge of what could have been is not pleasant when you have to come back to where you are."

"Yeah, that would really suck." I looked down at my comforter. Could I do this? He was right. It didn't seem like a big deal now, but it had the potential to be the biggest catch in the world. It would hurt if my alternate choices turned out to be great, and I had to give them all up.

I looked up at him. "It could really end up hurting, but I think that knowing would be better than not being sure. I accept that I've made poor choices. I have to live with them. I've been driving myself crazy thinking about things that I did or didn't do, so I'm not sure that's any better than knowing if it could be great. Kind of changing one sort of hell for another, you know?"

"You are clever. I like that. I knew I made a good decision with you. You want to do this, and you agree to the terms of the wishes I am offering you?"

"Yes. Three chances to go back to sometime in the past and live that time of my life over, but with different choices. I'll know all that I know right now, and I know that this is only temporary. We talk after the whole thing is done. "

"Got it in one. Good girl. All right, here's how it's going to happen. I'll give you a day to think this over, think of the one do-over you want first. I won't make you choose all three all at once. So think about where you want to go first, and then when you're sure, call for me, and we'll get this show on the road."

"How do I call you? On the phone? What?"

"Just speak my name. Say Dhameer and I'll be there in a flash."

"A flash, huh? What a surprise."

His eyes narrowed.

I hastened to smooth over my gaffe. "Seriously, Dhameer. Thanks for the day. I need to think about it."

"Of course. I want you to choose carefully. I wasn't lying to you when I said I like you and want to give you this chance. Like anything, it can be both bad and good, but it's what you want, so I am willing to help. Call me when you're ready."

He vanished in an instant, leaving only a dusting of glitter across the end of my comforter.

I leaned back against the pillows. Wow. That was some kind of crazy. I was some kind of crazy for agreeing to it all. He wasn't a burglar, and he had trotted out a small zoo and disappeared without needing a door of any sort. The chance to go back in time and do things differently didn't sound so crazy after spending a little time with Dhameer.

I decided to just go with it. If he was not a real-deal genie, only I would know. If he was, a world of possibilities had just opened up.

I snuggled back into the bed as I had been planning to do earlier, thinking on the moments that I really, really, really wanted to go back and relive.

***

The alarm went off, and I sat straight up, startled from sleep with the harsh buzzer. I looked at the clock to see how long I had been sleeping. It read 6:30.

18

Three Wishes

CHAPTER FOUR

Dhameer

Dhameer was meandering. He found the human woman Tabitha fascinating. He didn't normally see such an acceptance of one's faults in one so young. Of course, like most humans, she had taken it to the extreme and essentially wallowed in it. Nevertheless, too much responsibility was always preferable to none. Not that either are enjoyable for those around it.

He liked her. It was rare that he enjoyed his human wish recipients immediately. Normally it took some time for him to warm to them beyond their plight. The longer he had his freedom, the less he found reason to even look in on humans. As a result, he didn't offer wishes much anymore. They had to really call out to him, as Tabitha had. Generally humans were just so…human.

He shifted his path to avoid a flock of birds. He loved being able to fly whenever he chose. Today was one such day. Beautiful and sunny, it was a glorious day for a djinn to be alive, particularly for a free djinn such as himself.

A thought hooked him and dragged him to a halt. He hovered motionless, listening. Like Tabitha, he could hear the thoughts as though the one thinking them was shouting from the rooftops.

Two in the same week! This was a treat. He moved closer to the building below to see if he could find the person thinking. He flew above the building several times…listening, first here, and then…ah. There it was. He moved down to the rooms and shamelessly eavesdropped. He kept himself invisible. Much more interesting this way. Much less hassle, as well.

As he listened, his disbelief and amazement grew. How could this be? He hadn't planned on it, but it looked like he'd have two recipients at the same time.

Apartment 4C

The papers lay in his lap. It was over. Until the moment he'd opened the envelope, it hadn't seemed real. Not really. Not even after he'd moved out of the house they'd bought and fixed up together.

Not when he looked for her in these rooms, or in the kitchen, or humming in the shower, or snoring gently beside him when he finally turned off his bedside light. She wasn't there. Now with the papers, she never would be.

He poked at his feelings, as though he was poking at a sore tooth, testing to see if it really hurt. It did, but not in the way he thought it would. Or the way it should? He didn't know.

She'd said they weren't right together anymore. He'd hated to hear the words, but she was right. They weren't. He looked again at the papers in his lap. They didn't tell him anything he didn't already know.

So now what? He had his career. After all this time, though, he wasn't sure he wanted to continue. There was the offer to come home. He always had a job waiting back there. Maybe that was it. He needed to move, get out of this bland little apartment and work on forging a new direction for himself.

What did he want? In spite of joining the ranks of the divorced, he still believed in love. Just because he hadn't loved many —his thoughts flew to college, before he'd met his wife.

Tibby. Her real name was Tabitha. He'd found that out later, and not from her. He'd only known her as Tibby.

Tibby. What would his life be like if she'd said yes? He'd often wondered that. He wished she had, particularly as he'd obviously married the wrong person. Not that he could be sure Tibby was right. Just that he'd had a feeling about her that he'd never felt for anyone else. Maybe he should look her up, now that he was single.

Just as he was thinking about how to do that without coming across like the biggest stalker ever, he was blinded by a flash. He covered his eyes, and just as suddenly, the room went dark again.

He lowered his arms. There, in front of him, sat a man. Well, he looked kind of like a man. But not entirely. For one thing, he was covered in glitter. Could you get glitter paint like that? He wasn't sure. The guy didn't have a shirt, just a lot of glitter. For another…he peered more closely at his uninvited guest.

He didn't seem to have legs.

"No, I don't." The man spoke.

"What?" He looked up. "Who are you? How in the hell did you get in here? You need to leave, and I won't call the cops. Just get the hell out, and we'll call it a day." Normally, an intruder would have him searching for his weapon, but he found that he was too tired to make the effort. He just wanted to be alone.

"No, you don't. If you truly wanted to be alone, you wouldn't be lost in the past, wishing for something that never happened."

"What the—are you reading my mind?"

The man sighed. "I am. I'm a djinn. My name is Dhameer. I'm here to offer you the chance you're lamenting, if you wish it."

"What are you talking about?" This made no sense. Part of him knew he needed to call the cops or take a swing at this weird fuck, but it was as though he couldn't move.

"The girl. The girl I heard you thinking about. Do you want to try it again?"

"Wait. Wait just a damn minute." He was finally able to stand, and he moved quickly towards the painted man, ready to knock him out and call the cops.

Dhameer raised a hand, and he found that he was frozen.

"If you don't want the gift I'm offering you, just say so. I'll be out of here in a flash. But think for a moment with something other than your caveman senses. I am offering you a chance to go back, to live again that time in your life when the girl could have been part of your life, and this time, she'll say yes."

That got his attention.

"What do you mean, she'll say yes?"

Dhameer looked at him. "If I release you, will you sit and talk with me calmly, rather than trying to attack me?"

"Hey, I'm not the one that raided a craft store and broke into someone else's place."

"Semantics. I'm offering you a second chance. Do you want it or not?"

"How are you going to make that happen?"

"Humans. You never listen. I will tell you again. I am a djinn. My name is Dhameer. What you know as a genie. I grant wishes. Only ones that interest me, that I want to grant."

"Wait, wait, you live in a lamp?"

Dhameer rolled his eyes. "Disney ought to be shot. No, I do not live in a lamp. I live where I choose. I am beholden to none. I only grant wishes to those I choose. I am choosing you to give a wish."

"Don't I get three?"

"You get whatever I offer. The offer is about to disappear. Once more, do you want this wish? Do you want a second chance with the girl?"

Suddenly he could move. He sat back in his chair. "You'll send me back to when I offered Tibby a chance with me?"

"I will."

"And this time she'll say yes?"

The djinn's brow furrowed. "I am fairly certain."

"What do you mean? Why aren't you completely certain?"

"Because you humans and your nature make nothing one hundred percent predictable. Not ever. So I am fairly confident she'll say yes, but I cannot guarantee it."

"Okay, so let's say she does. What then?" He couldn't believe he was entertaining this idea, or this guy, or that he hadn't called the cops.

"Then you go forward with her new decision."

"I gotta live that part of my life over?"

"Indeed you do. No way out of it."

"What if she says no?"

Dhameer shrugged. "Then you get to relive those years with the wisdom you have now."

"Why is it I won't end up back here?" He didn't really know if he wanted to. Even without the chance for Tibby, reliving life from that point on could be interesting. Maybe even great.

"Because that's the way this works. You'll just go on, younger, with your extra wisdom and life experience. Is she really worth the effort? That is what you should be asking yourself now."

That made him shut up. Was she worth it? What did he really know about her? Lots of flirting, but when he made his move, nothing came of it. They laughed a great deal, and he just knew there was something special about her, but he'd been shot down when he tried to pursue it. A boyfriend. That was it. She had a boyfriend.

"Is that really your big regret from the past? I don't want to waste my efforts."

"Calm your glitter, genie. I'm thinking!"

"So I hear," Dhameer muttered.

He ignored the snark and considered. This was kind of a big deal, getting a chance to go back and do a part of his life over. And with everything he knew now! It was like a lottery ticket, really. So what if Tibby didn't work out? It would suck, but he'd finally know. And then he'd get to move on far smarter than he'd been at that age. But damn, he hoped she said yes this time. He'd always regretted that she hadn't. If he were honest, he'd married his now ex-wife because she had a spark of what he'd seen in Tibby.

"Yes."

"Yes, what? I need you to be specific."

"Yes. I want to go back to when I took a chance with Tibby, and this time, I want to get that chance."

"You agree to move on with life even if she doesn't agree?"

"Absolutely."

"Very well. I need you to think about her, and think about that night—"

"How do you know it was at night?"

Dhameer just looked at him.

"Oh. Right. Okay. Sorry, please continue."

"Thank you. Think about that night, and all the details you can remember."

He closed his eyes. Lost himself in the memories from that night. When he opened his eyes, he looked down. He was wearing the same thing he'd worn that night. He looked up. Same place. And in front of him, looking a little nervous, was Tibby.

Dhameer

He smiled, looking at the man in front of him. This had never happened before. He knew this would be one of Tibby's wishes. He could hear her thoughts, and he knew. He knew she was going to take the chance with this man, and he just couldn't believe the coincidence in running across him. When he thought about it, he'd never heard of this occurring with any other djinn, not ever before.

This was going to be fun to watch.

CHAPTER FIVE

Tibby

I rubbed my eyes, looking at the clock again. 6:30. It couldn't be. That would mean the entire meeting with Dhameer had been nothing more than a dream. The thought made me tear up. I wanted these wishes, these do-overs. God damn it! I wanted the chance to make something different of myself and of my life.

In my apparent dream, which seemed so real, I had committed to the idea of getting a do-over. To find that it was only a dream…I felt like someone had rolled over me in a tank.

I flopped back onto the bed, wiping away tears. I was surprised at how upsetting this was. I couldn't seem to stop the tears from welling up and spilling down my cheeks onto the pillow. I lay there until I couldn't stand the alarm anymore, and got up and turned it off. I felt battered. I couldn't work today. I grabbed the phone and called X to let him know I'd be delayed with the work he wanted done. I didn't call off much so he had no problem with giving me a sick day. Once the call was done, I crawled back into bed and cried as though someone had just died.

I stayed in bed most of the morning. I got up a few times to tend to the calls of nature, and thirst, and to see if there was actually a pee spot on my floor—there wasn't—but other than that, I didn't move. All morning, I thought about what I would like to have a chance to do over, what would be the top choice of my list. Towards the afternoon, I got tired of myself, and got up and grabbed my laptop. Even though it seemed as though I was in some kind of alternate dimension, I wanted to look up djinn, and see what the legends had to say about them. More importantly, how had I fallen for that line of bullshit? I wasn't drunk, or on any meds.

In Arabic lore, they were essentially fallen angels—given to mischief, attempting to possess men, and general troublemaking. Most of the sites I found referenced these sorts of stories. In Roman legend, they were spirits responsible for the development of man, a guiding spirit, if you will. The legend that I was familiar with came down to the Disney representation, which had its basis in Arabic folklore, although the actions of that genie seemed to be more of the Roman variety. Most of the Arabic tales had djinn being malicious and wont to trick humans for their own gain or amusement.

Well. That didn't bode well for me. Since it had all been a dream, I guess I dodged a bullet. Somehow, that didn't make me feel better. I pushed my laptop aside and resumed feeling sorry for myself. In true ruminator fashion, I went back to what I would have liked to have a shot at going back to, what times I would like to have changed in my past.

Not partying like I was some sort of rock star for

five or six years would be one. I couldn't see myself going back to the first time I drank to excess though. I didn't even really remember when that was, to be honest. It would have stopped me from lots of bad, bad, men, and wasted time on said bad, bad men, but really, there wasn't a beginning point to all that.

Because of my interesting childhood, I always felt I was never good enough, and that I had no one to depend on but myself. As an adult, I knew that wasn't true, since I had made something like peace with my family over the upsets I had carried for so long. It didn't change my ingrained behavior though. I chose men who were not truly available, who lied, who would use me, and deep down, I knew it. That sucked worst of all. I knew what I set myself up for, did it anyway, and then moped and sulked around as though I had no ability to influence my own life.

Once more, I thanked God for X. He saved me, in more ways than one. He put up with all my bullshit, and offered me a safe place to land.

What sucked even more was that finally, I'd thought I had a chance to do something different, and had decided to get off my ass and do it. Then I wake up, and it's all been a dream!

As pathetic as that all sounds when laid out like this, I just didn't see one spot that would be considered a crossroads. That left me with thinking over the moments where I knew I was making a choice of some kind. Usually the wrong one. In spite of the fact I was not proud of such moments and regretted being part of them, they weren't what I would spend a wish on.

I did this for the rest of the afternoon, going back and forth over what were the points in time where I could *really* effect some sort of change. I ignored the fact that it didn't appear to have happened. Finally, as the sun was going down, and my room was getting dark, I made up my mind. It might have been a dream, and this could be a prelude to another day crying in bed, but I was going to give it a shot. If I was wrong, and it was all a dream, as I said before, no one would know I was being silly but me.

I got out of bed, and tidied myself a little. I looked up at the ceiling, and sent out a little plea for hope. Hope that I wasn't being a delusional fool. Took a deep breath, and opened my mouth.

"Dhameer."

He stood, sort of, in front of me.

"Decided, have you?"

"What the hell was the point of putting me through all this today? Was it just a dream?"

"Yes and no. It was a dream, but it really happened. Call it a little test. I wanted to see if you would call on me anyway."

I glared. "I can see why genies are associated with maliciousness."

"I prefer the term 'djinn'. Most of us shouldn't be. Humans have long been willing to put poor choice off on something or someone other than themselves. An evil spirit is a winning lottery ticket in that respect. As I told you, I make my own decisions and choose carefully whom I grant wishes to. Part of that is seeing if you are capable of having a little faith, some belief when it seems impossible. Rather like an application. You, Toots, have passed. You ready to head down memory lane?"

I nodded. "Yes. I know where I want to go first. It was—" He cut me off.

"No need to tell me. Close your eyes and see it in your mind. What you were wearing, how you looked, where you were, summon up all the details you can." He was quiet then, and I closed my eyes and brought it back.

I was at the neighbor's house. My hometown had a good sized college in it. Our neighbor was an alumna and had a son who was a current student. The wife half of the couple liked to host parties and invite all her son's friends over. It was a big football game, an away game, so a ton of people had come over to watch the game. My family was always invited, as my parents were friends with them. They didn't know the horrors that happened in my house daily. My parents hid it well. The son and I got along, but it was casual. One of his friends was a different story. Oh, Rick. Rick Montevaldo.

I had met Rick the end of my freshman year of high school. He was finishing up his freshman year of college. He hung out at the house a lot, and so we got to see one another frequently as my parents socialized with the neighbors regularly. And boy, did the neighbors like to socialize. Looking back, that socializing may have been why my parents got along with them. Drunk birds of a feather, and all that. I was just so involved in getting through my life I couldn't see that my normal might not have been normal to everyone else.

In spite of trying to make sure my parents didn't disgrace us all, Rick and I flirted like mad at these parties. Our friendship grew out of that. Since I didn't have a driver's license, he would take me out shopping and to run errands. I looked forward to those times. I had a boyfriend, and while Rick and I flirted, he never seemed serious because he was a jokey kind of guy.

Something changed in our respective junior years. He had taken a violent dislike to my boyfriend which was, in hindsight, a good call. Things were rocky with the boyfriend and me, so that night, rather than go out with him, I went with my parents to the neighbors. I was hoping Rick was there, and he was.

The game didn't go well. The home team got stomped. Everyone was drinking their sorrows away. That was back when I was a Serious Athlete, and wouldn't dream of drinking. I was down in the basement, watching a movie, and getting another soda, when Rick found me.

CHAPTER SIX

He was drunk. I hadn't seen him like this before. Since I didn't drink, it was a little scary. I was standing right next to the wall, and he leaned over and put his hand on the wall behind my head.

"Open your eyes, Tibby, and take it from here, Toots." I heard in a whisper in my ear.

"Hey, Slickster, what's up?" Slick Rick was his nickname. I didn't know why, but I had appropriated it and made it a little bit mine.

"Been lookin' for you," he said.

"I'm right here," I said with a little raise of my eyebrows, flirting like we always did.

"Good. I wanna talk to you. "

"Okay. You want to sit down? We can talk."

"No, talk right here. So I want to ask you to my formal, but I can't."

"What are you talking about?" I guessed this was something to do with his fraternity.

"My formal. For my…for my fraternity." Woo boy. He was drunk. No wonder he'd scared me. Too much like my daily life. I didn't say anything, and he continued. "It's comin' up soon, and I want to ask you. But I know your dad won't like it. Cus' I would take you, and people would say, oh, hi, what year are you? And you would say, a junior, and when they asked what school, you'd say your high school, and I'm just too old for you. And your dad would kill me. Shoot at me, maybe."

We were coming up to the crossroads. Just as it did all those years ago, I could feel my heart pounding. I'd always wanted to hear something like this from Rick, and now I was. Sure, he was drinking. But unlike my parents, he hadn't ever hurt me. I didn't know whether this was the booze or for real, and I wouldn't until I let this go on. Besides, if he was like my parents, I was better equipped to handle him. A knee right to the crotch and I'd be outta there. I took a breath, and calmed myself. A drunk guy, and especially this guy, was nothing to be afraid of. Not everyone was my parents. Part of me was pissed at how much damage they'd done. Time for that with the shrink later.

"I don't think he would shoot you, Rick. I don't think you're too old, either." Like my dad would even notice. I resisted the urge to roll my eyes.

"I am. I'm too old. I wish you were jus' a little bit older. Then I wouldn't get shot, an' no one would be calling me cradle robber."

"No one calls you that." I looked at him a bit more closely. Now that I was in this, and not just remembering, he wasn't as drunk as I'd thought.

"Yeah, they do. They keep saying, when you gonna finally rob that cradle? You've been rocking it for two years, Slick, time to make a move. I wanna make a move, I just want to take you out, go places, hold your hand, and go out. But it's hard. I like you a lot. I jus' wanna date you, like a normal guy. Beat your boyfriend's ass. He's an ass. You're too good for him. Asshole." He leaned down, shaking his head.

Wow, I had really exaggerated how drunk he was in my memory. Seeing him now, he seemed somewhere between tipsy and drunk. What a difference nine years makes. When I had found myself here before, it had made me uncomfortable, and I hadn't really listened. I was planning my getaway. My sister had just come downstairs, and was looking at me with the *do you need help?* look. Before, I had given her the *Save me!* crazy eyes, and she had come over and helped me scoot away. This time, I shook my head a little, and she walked into the other room where a bunch of people were playing pool. Change of choice number one.

I stood a little closer to him, looking up at him, making him look at me.

"You don't need to beat Dave's ass," I said. "We're about over anyway. Waste of time. I'll just dump him and be done with it. I like you, too. I have for a long time. I just didn't think you were really interested. Let me talk to my dad, and I'll stop him from getting a gun, okay?"

"How could you think that? It was totally obvious," he protested. Clearly I had been missing a lot of signals.

"Not to me. You're older, hot, and way out of my league. I just thought you had fun flirting with me."

"I wanna do a lot more than flirt," he said. He leaned down and kissed me. It was kind of clumsy. Clumsy groping was another fun side of semi-drunken declarations.

I put my arms around his neck and kissed him back. I kissed him pretty fiercely, nearly biting his lip. I backed away, wanting to apologize, but he pulled me up hard, close to him, and kissed me before I could get a word out. It was far less clumsy than before. Holy hell, I could feel it all the way to my toes.

He broke off kissing me as a loud cheer started behind us. Jake, my neighbor's son, and a bunch of his friends were applauding enthusiastically. Rick looked a little embarrassed, and took my hand, and said, "C'mon, let's get out of here." He towed me towards the stairs, ignoring all the catcalls coming from his friends. I have to admit, I was blushing. Nobody sounded hateful. He was telling the truth. People had seen his signals. God. Teenagers were really blind. Maybe he was right, and this four year age difference was too much.

Wait. It was actually a five year age difference in my favor. I was really twenty-six to his twenty-one. I wasn't the seventeen year old who had run from this before. That calmed my momentary panic. I looked around, paying more attention to where he was taking me than I had when in the throes of rising panic. We were upstairs in the main living room, but on the edge of the room. He leaned down to me.

"There's your dad. Can you go get him? I wanna talk to him now."

"Are you sure that's a good idea? You're a little toasty." I was worried how my dad, also probably a little toasty, might react.

"I want to get this in the open. I figure if you're standing with him, I won't get shot right away."

I had to snicker to myself. He had pegged my dad pretty accurately. Dad was very protective of my sister and I when he was sober. No doubt because he knew exactly what men were capable of. He hadn't liked one of my boyfriends yet. He hated Dave.

Called him the Grab Ass, because he swore Dave had groped me right in front of him. I had never recalled such a thing, but in hindsight, Dave was an ass. Everything that happened once we broke up showed that.

Anyway, time to focus on the situation at hand. "Okay, I'll go get him. You sure you want to talk to him?"

"Yes. I've wanted to talk to him for the last two years. Don't want to wait any longer." His face was determined. I stood on my toes and kissed his cheek, and then walked over to where my dad was sitting. He was talking with some of our other neighbors, and I waited for a lull in the conversation. That was probably new too. I was pretty self-centered as a teenager.

"You need something, honey?" He looked up at me. I could see that he'd been drinking moderately. It was hard not to shake him and tell him to clean the fuck up. *Stop, Tibby. You're a teenager, and you need something from him. He'll want to be the great dad in public. Act nice and ask nicely.*

"Dad, can you come here a minute? I need to talk to you."

He looked alarmed. "Is everything okay?"

"Yes, it's fine. But I really need to talk to you. It won't take long. Please?"

"Well, okay." He got up from the couch.

"Thank you," I said to him. I looked over at the other two men. "Thanks for letting me steal him for a minute." My dad looked at me with a faint air of surprise. Hmmm. Apparently my manners had not been stellar at the time, either. What a nice side effect of the do-over—seeing what an ill-mannered snot you were. I shrugged that off and took my dad's arm. It made me wonder if my dad put on manners too. A thought hit me. Maybe they weren't the assholes I'd thought of them as. I needed to look at this through my eyes, not my teenaged eyes. *Stop it! Focus on the task at hand!*

"Could we just step into the other room?" I asked.

"Sure, honey. You sure everything's okay?"

I laughed. "Quit worrying. I just need to talk to you, and I'd rather get it over with than wait."

"You're making me nervous. Are you pregnant?" He hissed, and tightened his grip on my arm.

CHAPTER SEVEN

"Oh my god, not even close!" I pulled my arm from him, giving him a *what the fuck* glare. Figures. We didn't have an audience now. We passed by where Rick was standing, and I angled my head at him to let him know to come with us. I went into the front room, which, since it had no TV, was empty of people.

"Have a seat," I said, steering him towards an arm chair. Rick came in behind me, sort of hesitantly. Once my dad sat down, I took Rick's hand, and sat on the sofa across from where my dad was sitting. It forced Rick to sit down with me. I stole a glance at him from the corner of my eye. In spite of his earlier determination, he looked nervous. I could understand that. My dad could make me nervous too.

"What's this all about?" Daddy asked. He looked from me to Rick, and I could see the dots connecting for him. At least he'd put the *I'm a good dad* face back on. Plus, I wasn't sitting near enough for him to get hold of me.

"Dad, I've liked Rick for a long time."

"I know that." Oh hell. He sounded like his gruff self. The same man who had met my first boyfriend when both the guy and I were thirteen, and waved a shotgun in the poor guy's face. Add to that an exaggerated drawl, and my dad asking the guy if he knew what shotguns were used for, and you had the shortest relationship in history. That particular boyfriend was gone before he walked out of the door ten minutes later.

"He likes me too."

"I …like her a lot, sir," Rick said.

Whoa. He didn't sound completely steady. Perhaps he was more intoxicated than I thought. In spite of my dad being a drunk, he was pretty judgmental about others who drank. I stifled my sigh. I needed to get through this. *C'mon Tibby. You're twenty-six, not seventeen. And this is not as horrible as you remember. Handle this like an adult!*

"You do, huh?" said Dad.

"Yes. I want to ask you if I can take her out and date her. I know I'm older, but I've known Tibby for a couple of years, and I don't care about the age."

"Course you don't. She's seventeen, hasn't been around like you." Crap. Dad was getting all defensive.

I laughed, trying to keep it light. "Dad, I've been dating since I was thirteen. You've scared every one of them. Rick just told me how he feels about me. Then he told me he wanted to talk to you right away. I think that's, well, pretty honorable." *Oh, please please please don't screw this up because you've been drinking, Dad!*

Dad looked at me. "It is, I guess. It's the decent thing to do. Or the smart thing," he said, turning to glare at Rick.

Good grief. Maybe there was a reason I didn't make this decision back then. I am not sure I could have fielded all this with any kind of grace. I would have gotten all huffy and snippy with my dad, adding it to the list of shit he did to ruin my life, which would have probably doomed the whole thing. Thinking about things that way cheered me immensely. I was already in a better place than I'd been. It wasn't just because I'd said yes to Rick, either. I might actually come out of this better off. I took a deep breath and banished my nerves.

"If there are dastardly motives, I'll figure it out. I'm not stupid."

"Why now?" Dad asked Rick.

"I saw the opportunity and decided to risk it," Rick said.

"She's still in high school. You have the same rules as anyone else who goes out with her. You respect that, and I'll give you a chance."

Rick reached across and shook my dad's hand. "Thank you, sir. I'll follow the rules." He was smiling. Amazingly, he didn't seem as tanked as before.

"All right now. Go on, and let me talk to Tibby."

Rick smiled at me, and gave me a hug, and then got up and left. I watched him go, loving the way he looked, and then turned back to my dad. *No judgement,* I thought. *Be seventeen and thankful.*

"Thanks, Dad. I know he's older, but I have known him a while, he used to take me shopping, and never did anything that I would slap him for."

"You like him, so why would you slap him?"

"If he's creepy, or pushy, or whatever, I would have. Then I would have run like hell."

He stood up, pulling me up with him. "That's my girl. He's on probation. He's too old for you, but he does seem to care about you, and he had the guts to talk to me. That's more than Grab Ass ever did. Speaking of which, this mean you are going to can him?"

"Yeah. We are close to breaking up anyway. He's kind of a jerk."

"Knew that all along," Dad grumbled.

"Well, you have to let me make my own mistakes. You can be happy that now I'm admitting you're right."

"Glad I won't have to see his sucking up phony face anymore."

I laughed. "Hey, don't be shy. Tell me how you really feel."

"I have been telling you. Only now you're finally listening."

I hugged him. "Is it okay if I go now?" I couldn't be too adult.

"Yeah, get out of here. No sneaking off to any bedrooms, or I'll come and find you."

"Dad! I can't believe you think I would do that!"

"I know my kids," he said.

"Well, maybe I am trying to change," I said in a snotty tone. Gee, thanks, Dad. *Stop! Stop it! Your parents are not the point here!*

"We'll see, kiddo. We'll see. Go find the guy. Stay out of anywhere dark."

I rolled my eyes at him and hurried out of the front room. I wasn't planning on going anywhere dark, but somewhere sparsely populated would be nice. I rounded the corner, and headed into the kitchen. Rick was standing there, talking to Jake in low tones. He looked up as I came in and his whole face lit up. Wow. Wow wow wow. That was really great to see. I couldn't remember the last time a man had looked like that when he saw me. I could feel my knees melting.

"Hey," I said.

"Hey," he said as he reached for me. His arm went around my waist, and he pulled me close to him. I leaned into him, and saw my dad heading back into the living room, sending a glare our way without breaking his stride. I rolled my eyes at him as he went past. Rick heaved a big sigh.

"I am so glad that's over," he said.

"That was smart of you. I know he respects that you came to him up front."

"I hope so. He carries a gun. He has a lot of guns. I would like to never have to see them."

Jake laughed and clapped Rick on the shoulder. "Well done, Slick. I'll just leave you to it," he said with a small leer, and he went to the basement door and down the stairs.

Once he disappeared, Rick turned to me and put his other arm around me. I had never really hugged him before. I couldn't believe how nice his chest felt. He rested his head on top of mine and just held me. We stood like that for several minutes, and then he leaned back.

"You need to tell Asshole tomorrow."

"You know tomorrow's Sunday, right? I might not see him. He does a lot of stuff with his family."

"Don't you usually talk every day?"

"Well, yeah. It seems kind of mean to break up over the phone."

"Who cares? He's an asshole. He deserves to get kicked to the curb over the phone."

"He probably does," I said, thinking of how Dave had reacted when I had broken up with him. He had spread all kinds of nasty tales about me, about how I was such a slut, all the things I would willingly do, that kind of shit. We hadn't even slept together, even though we had been dating for almost a year and a half. Rick was right. He was an asshole. And he had been an asshole for the rest of the year to me for daring to break up with him. Well, to hell with being courteous. If he was going to talk shit about me, I might as well go ahead and be the bitch he painted me as.

"You're right. He does. You know what? I'll call him right now."

"You will? Good. The sooner you tell him, the better." I made to walk to the kitchen phone, but he grabbed me and pulled me back to him. He took my face in his hands and kissed me. This time, he was a lot less clumsy. Once again, the kiss was a toe curler. It was going to be hard not dragging him off somewhere and shredding his clothes. With just a few kisses, he brought back all the intense feelings I had ever had for him. Only now, because I had gained a bit of wisdom about relationships, and the opposite sex, and sex in general, I knew how good this could be. I could love this guy. I'd suspected it before, but I knew it now. I was a twenty-six year old woman in a seventeen year old body. It had been some time since my last partner. I was going to have to go get on birth control. I didn't see myself holding out long.

"I can't call if you're kissing me," I said, smiling at him. "I'd rather be kissing you, but I need to get this out of the way."

"Okay, okay. Go. Talk to him for the last time." He looked a little surly.

I leaned towards him to whisper. "You're super sexy when you're jealous," I said.

"Go," he said, waving me towards the phone.

When I picked up the phone, I stopped. Shit. I didn't know the number! I closed my eyes, thinking, and let my fingers drift across the phone. I dialed a number and mentally crossed my fingers.

I couldn't believe it when Dave's mom answered the phone. That was pure, dumb luck. It took her a minute to collect him. They had a pool room at their house too, and Dave had told me some of the guys were going to come over and shoot pool and watch movies. With a start, I remembered that X hung out with Dave at times. Would he be there tonight?

"Hey. Babe." His mom must have told him it was me.

"Hey," I said.

"What's up? I thought you were next door at the game party."

"I am, I'm calling you from there."

"Are you okay? You sound weird."

"No, I'm not okay."

"What's wrong?" He asked.

"We've been arguing a lot," I said. "It seems like we do that more than anything else."

"Well, yeah," he said.

"I think that means something. I think we need to stop seeing each other." Boom. Done. I would have hemmed and hawed over this in high school.

"What? What are you talking about? We don't need to break up over this," he said.

Riiiiight, I said to myself. *Because who's going to take care of your Mr. Happy if we break up?* I stopped my internal bitch, because if I didn't, it would come out in the conversation. I kept remembering how people would drive by me as I walked home from school, taunting me with the things that Dave told them.

When it had happened, I had been so hurt, and a little afraid. It's scary, a car full of guys asking you if you'll give them blowjobs because Dave said you gave really good head. They never pulled that shit when I was with X, as he was quick with the fists in those days, but he couldn't watch out for me all the time. Thinking about it now made me angry. I already knew what he was going to do, so I would just end it, and then take care of him on Monday at school.

"I think we do. I think we both knew this was coming and have been avoiding it. I didn't want to face it, but I'm tired of all the fighting. I know you are, too, Dave. It's not fun. It's not fun to date someone you fight with all the time."

"There's someone else, isn't there? You are such a slut."

"All righty then. That's it for me being polite. I'm done, Dave. No coming back from that. I was right about you. Later, asshole." I slammed the phone down.

"What did he say?"

"Asked me if there was someone else and called me a slut."

"I'll beat his ass. Just say the word."

"No need. I can handle him. He's a punk. Don't worry about it."

"I'm going to take you to school and pick you up this week," he said. "He's a dick. I don't want him to hassle you."

"You would do that for me?" I said. I was really touched. It had been a long time since anyone had offered to make a chivalrous move on my behalf other than X.

"Of course I will. You're my girl, and no one gets

to call you a slut."

I leaned close to him and, lord help me, I practically purred. "You might get to call me a bad girl, if you're lucky." The crazy thing is, I KNOW I used to flirt with him like this. In high school, I had innuendo down to a tee. How had nothing ever happened?

He gave me a quick, hard kiss. "You gotta stop that. You're a terrible tease."

"Am I?" I was interested to see what he thought. While pulling it together, he was not sober, so he might be willing to be all honest and open.

"Are you kidding me? You've been driving me crazy since I met you. You are totally the biggest flirt I have ever met."

"I know, I am flirty, but I meant it with you." I looked up at him and batted my eyes at him.

"You better mean it only with me," he said. "I don't share well with others."

Hmmm. He looked rather serious. Did he have a really bad jealous streak? I smiled. "Good. I don't either."

"Yeah, but you've had a boyfriend since I met you. There's that guy you're always with too, what's his name? Excalibur?"

I laughed. "Xavier. We're just friends. Look at what happened now, Rick—all it took for me to be free was for you to tell me how you feel."

"It's about time. He wasn't good enough for you."

"I know. I didn't used to think that, but I know it now."

"I mean it, Tibby. I don't share. It's made me crazy watching you date that guy. That time he came over here looking for you, I nearly beat the crap out of him. Lucky for him that Jake stopped me."

"I always wondered why you were so angry about that. I know you guys had been drinking, but I always thought that he hadn't done anything to piss you off."

"Except be an asshole and still get to date you. He bothers you at all, you tell me, okay?"

"I will. But will you trust me that I can handle him? I already know that he's going to talk shit about me, call me names, that kind of thing. Let me deal with it. I'm a big girl, and I'm the one that needs to stomp him if he gets shitty." Not to mention X would help out in that department. Given Rick's jealousy, probably not a good thing to mention right this moment.

Rick looked at me with an odd look. "I bet you can. I know I'm kind of trashed," he ignored my very unladylike noise, "but you're different. It's like, I don't know, I always saw you one way, and you're still that way, but more. Never mind, that sounds completely stupid."

"No, it doesn't. Listen, I won't be so flirty, I'll keep all my wiles just for you. There is more to me. I bet there's more to you, too. You're no slouch when it comes to being all flirty and practically indecent." I mock glared. "And you're giving me hell? I wasn't talking to myself, you know." I was going to need to find the teenaged me again. How the hell that was going to happen automatically, I didn't know. Thankfully, he wasn't entirely sober now, so I still had a little wiggle room. I could still be Older Tibby right now, and he would chalk it up to impressions made while drinking.

"It's 'cause you drive me crazy."

"Oh, no! You don't get to blame this one on me!" I laughed at him.

"No, seriously, you do. Don't you realize how sexy you are?"

"Not really. No one takes me seriously. I don't think I really want them to."

He kissed me at that. "I do," he said.

"That's because it was always real for you, Rick," I said. "Always. I have liked you since the first time I met you."

"So you'll go to formal with me?" He asked.

"Do you want me to not mention where I go to school?" I asked.

"Now that we're doing more than just flirting, I don't think anyone will even ask."

"Does it really bother you?" I really wanted to know. I didn't think he was shallow, but this might peg him as such.

"Yeah. I wish you were older. I feel kind of like a dirty old man, especially since I met you when you were fifteen and I was nineteen. You're still in high school. I don't know, it's like I wish you had a chance to get out and meet more people. Then you would know that you really wanted to be with me."

"You are such an honorable guy," I said. I knew this was somewhat out of character for the teenaged me, but I had to tell him. "I have been dating other people. I dated a couple of guys before Dave, and none of them were ever as nice to me as you've always been. Don't worry about it. I want to be with you."

"I am so glad to hear you say that," he said, giving me a hug.

"You don't know how happy and excited I was

when you talked to me downstairs," I said.

"Really? You looked nervous."

"I was, a little. Then I thought, this is what you've wanted to hear from this guy for like two years, what are you waiting for?"

"I meant it, when I said I…liked you a lot," he said. His face was very serious. Nevertheless, I didn't think that was exactly what he wanted to say. I let it be.

"So did I. I like you a lot, too. I have for a long time." He didn't know the half of it.

We eventually went back into the front room and sat on the couch holding hands, my legs in his lap. We talked the rest of the night, cuddling and kissing. I cannot tell you how much I wanted to just jump on him. It was amazing to be with him, to see what might have happened had I been brave enough. He'd already noticed the difference, though, so I kept my hormones reined in.

CHAPTER EIGHT

As promised, Rick took me to school every day that week and picked me up after school every afternoon. He even relented and gave X a ride home a couple of times. I was glad to see that X liked Rick, and Rick understood when I told him that we were just friends. Dave, as he did before, started talking trash about my sexual skills. Unlike before, I didn't cry and huddle in shame. I held my head high, and rolled my eyes as I heard about it. When one of the bitchy, gossipy chicks I knew came to tell me what she had heard a whole three days after we broke up, I laughed in her face. I was alone, of course. She was shocked. Her mouth hung open a little.

"Doesn't that bother you?" she asked.

"No, Terry, it doesn't. He's pissed off I broke up with him over the phone. He's all butt-hurt and has to take it out on someone. Why would I care what he says? So he's saying I give good head? So what? It means I cared enough about him to try and make the times we were intimate special, even though he would never reciprocate. It's one of the reasons I ended it. He is so completely mean and selfish."

"He's totally calling you a slut. Says you've been sleeping with Xavier this whole time." She looked kind of mulish. Oooh, this was fun.

"I'll bet he hasn't said that to Xavier." She didn't respond. I tapped my lip with my finger. "Let me guess. I beg for it all the time, too." Her eyebrows went up, which told me I was on the mark, but she stayed quiet.

"You want to know something about him? We never, ever had sex. He didn't believe in sex before marriage. He always wanted a blow job and would get offended if I said no. But he wouldn't reciprocate in *any* way," I stressed the word any so she didn't miss my meaning. "It was against his religion, or his sense of entitlement, or whatever. He would give me hints that he…" I paused to sink the knife in good. "He just couldn't handle it." I gave a shrug so she would see what I thought of such a statement. "All I know is that I loved and cared about him and tried to do things to make him feel good, and he didn't do the same. And now, he's saying I'm a slut. It just makes me so much happier that I dumped his ass. He's a selfish pig, and I don't give a shit what he says." I closed my locker with a bang. "I've got to go, Terry. Rick will be waiting for me."

"Who's Rick?" She asked.

I smiled broadly. "The man I have really wanted for the past two years. You should come with me and see him. He's totally gorgeous. Then you can see why I don't care what Dave says or who he says it to." I walked away, and she caught up with me, as I knew she would.

"So where did you meet him?"

"He goes to college, and he's friends with my neighbors. We hang out with them a lot, so I used to see him over there with his friend. He finally told me that he really liked me. He's a lot older though, which is why it took him a while to talk to me."

"Really? How old is he?"

"He's twenty one, a junior. He has one more year before he graduates. You know what's really cool?"

She shook her head.

"My parents love him. Even though he's older, and that would normally piss them off, they know him and really like him. They haven't liked any of my boyfriends before, and they totally hated Dave. My dad thought he was a smart-ass and a dick. Since he's talking shit and being as mean and as big of a jerk as possible, my dad was right."

She didn't say anything, which was fine as we had come out the front door. As promised, Rick was leaning on his car, waiting for me.

"Oh, hey, there's Rick. I gotta go. Nice talking with you," I said, walking away. I gave her a little wave and then promptly forgot about her as I reached Rick. He grabbed me and picked me up in a big hug. I kissed him, and he hugged me tighter.

"How's things?" He asked.

"Let's go and I'll tell you all about it," I said with a grin. I turned around and saw that Terry was still standing there watching us. It almost looked like her mouth was hanging slightly open "Bye, Terry!" I called, waving. Rick held the car door open for me, and I got in. He closed it and was around the car and next to me with lightning speed. I glanced out of the corner of my eye and could see Terry still there. *Good. Now go tell everybody.* The thought made me smile. Then I put her out of my mind. There were better things at hand.

I leaned over and kissed Rick, and he took my

face in his hands and gave me one of his toe curlers.

"Let's get the hell outta here," he said.

"Let's," I agreed.

We drove to my favorite ice cream shop. Over cones, I told him about all the rumors people were just so happy to tell me all about. He was angry.

"I am so going to beat his ass. I can't believe he is saying that about you."

"I can. He's a selfish, bratty little boy. You don't have to beat him up. I just ruined him."

"How?"

I told him about my conversation with Terry, and all the things I had informed her of. As he listened, he started laughing.

"You did just totally ruin him. He doesn't have a chance of ever getting a blowjob again. When does he graduate?" Rick laughed some more. "That's going to be his only shot. To get the hell out of school and go somewhere no one knows him!" He leaned forward, laughing harder. Then he sobered, and glared like Dave stood across the room from us. "It won't help that he's saying all these things about you, either. I can beat his ass and settle this shit."

"I hope so. I thought I would be so upset or ashamed. But I'm not. I'm angry and since he opened the door, I'm going to walk right in. No need for you to beat him up. He's already done." Boom. I had just vanquished one of the demons of my high school years. Even though Dave graduated a year before I did, all the things he said about me had lingered on. With this little five minute conversation with a gossip, I negated years of his crap. He was graduating, and all the shit he'd thrown would stick with him and not even be an issue for me. I could see it already.

"Remind me to stay on your good side," Rick said.

"You are part of my good side. Being with you has made me totally brave."

"And your dad thought I would be such a bad influence," he leered at me, waggling his eyebrows.

"Well, you probably will be. I'll be pretty happy about it, though, so ignore what my dad says."

"As much as I would like to say otherwise, you don't have to worry about that. Not right now, anyway," he said. "Later, for sure. There's no rush though."

"What was that I read in one of my trashy romance novels? Oh yeah. 'Anticipation heightens pleasure.'" I grinned. "I wouldn't mind seeing if that's true."

"You're gonna kill me," he said, shaking his head.

"If you're lucky," I said. He looked up to look at me, and I slowly licked my ice cream spoon.

"I am," he said.

***

It was actually another two months before we finally hit the wall of tolerance, and anticipation gave way to action. We had been sitting in his room, watching TV. He lived in a big, shabby, old Victorian that was close to his school. As usual, we were both all touchy feely, but not going beyond that. I realized, with a shock, that he was waiting for me. So much for age being able to give me all the answers. I decided to take one for the team and make the first move.

I entwined his hand with mine, and then lifted it up. I let go of his hand and started tracing his fingers with my thumb, one by one. I felt him move next to me, and I glanced up to see him looking down at me. I could see the heat in his eyes. But he was still waiting. I'll be honest, I wanted him to pounce on me, but I was going to have to lead him to it.

I gave him a small smile, and then looked away from him and back to his hand. Slowly, deliberately, I pulled his hand towards me, and then very slowly took his index finger in my mouth. I closed my mouth around it, and then pulled his hand out, sucking gently on it as I did so.

I didn't even have time to look at him before he had me on my back kissing me fiercely. He was rubbing his hands up and down my body, which was, to my dismay, still fully clothed. I had hoped for some shredded clothing. He's so nice, I thought. I love that.

So I pulled on his shirt, tugging it over his head. He raised himself up on his arms, and took the back of his shirt, pulled it off, and tossed it to the floor. I reached for his shorts, unbuttoning the button and pulling down the zipper as he kissed me again. He shrugged out of them. While he was doing that, I unbuttoned my top, and he pulled it over my head. I started to take my skirt off, but he stopped me. Reaching under it, he tugged off my panties. Oooh, I thought. Nice.

He took my bra from me and tossed it to the floor, then he leaned back, looking at me.

"What?" I resisted the urge to cover my chest. It was unnerving, the way he looked at me.

"You are so beautiful," he whispered, reaching down to run his hands from my hair to my breasts and then down to my hips and legs. "Even more than I imagined, and trust me, I've been imagining a lot."

I pushed myself up to twine an arm around his neck, pulling him towards me for a kiss. I kissed him hard, biting his lip, starting to lift myself off the bed to him. He stopped me.

"I want this to be special."

"It is special," I whispered. "You're my first." Which was true.

Whatever he'd been expecting from me, that wasn't it. His mouth fell open, and he let go of me a little.

"What? You're kidding me."

I shook my head, feeling shy, even as my twenty-six year old self. "No. I never slept with anyone before this. I wasn't ready."

"Why didn't you tell me? Why are we just having this conversation now?" This was so sweet that tears sprung to my eyes.

He sounded upset. I needed to head that off at the pass. Guilt wasn't going to do anyone any good here.

"Rick, this isn't rocket science. We both want it so bad we're about to explode. I've been having sex dreams about you for years. Now it's time to make it real."

That distracted him. "Years?"

I smiled, hoping I looked sexy. "Well, yeah! I told you, I've liked since I met you."

"Oh, man. I don't want to screw this up."

I could see the concern and nervousness on his face. I hastened to reassure him. "You're not going to." I knew I wasn't his first, and let's face it, I wasn't truly seventeen and clueless. "Now stop worrying and start making love to me. I can't wait another second longer."

With that, I laid back on the bed, and waited. I found that in spite of being the older me, I felt breathless and my stomach fluttered. I hoped he wouldn't be disappointed in me. I appreciated his concern, and it made me weepy as hell with love for him, but damn. This was one beautiful man in front of me, naked and ready. It had been too long since I'd seen one of those. It was time to get down to brass tacks. I stifled a laugh that encompassed both nerves and excitement at the practical nature of my thoughts.

I was very late getting home that night. I ended up with a week's grounding for blowing off my curfew. It was worth it.

***

We dated the rest of the summer and all through our respective senior years. A week before graduation, he asked me if we could get together one night. While he was done with his finals, I still had two to go and was studying like mad. I agreed to meet him and went over to his place after I had studied for a couple of hours.

He was sitting on the front porch waiting for me. He stood as I walked up the steps and scooped me up. It was his way of greeting me, and I loved it.

"Hey, you," I said.

"Hey you," he answered.

"What's going on? I see you all the time. Why the special invite?"

His eyes changed, and his whole body appeared to stiffen.

Oh holy hell. I caught myself before I said anything else. Why didn't I see this coming? This was the breakup scene. I took a deep breath and tried to steel myself. Even though Dhameer had told me it wasn't permanent, I had been here a long time. He hadn't yanked me from this yet. I often wondered what was going on in my old life, but this life was so much better, I didn't care. I was with Rick, X and I were still friends—there was nothing else I wanted. Things were even better with my parents, somewhat.

Maybe this was it for me in this go-round. Maybe I'd used up this do-over. Rick and I were on the cusp of going different ways. Maybe...maybe...I looked up as he came closer.

Rick looked normal, not all stiff and deer-caught-in-the-headlights as he had a moment before. He took my hand and drew me to him, putting his arms around me, stopping all the thoughts racing through my head. However, he still looked sort of cagey. Well, it was amazing while it lasted. I was glad to have had the chance to be with him. If I went back now, I knew that I had changed. For the better.

"I wanted to talk to you, and my roommates are out tonight. It'll be quiet most of the night."

"Until they come home roaring drunk," I said.

"Well, yeah, but hopefully we'll be done talking by then."

Yup. This was it.

He took my hand and led me up to his room. Crap crap crap. This was our place together, and now I was going to remember it as the dump-o-rama.

When we went into his room, he had all the candles lit. We both liked the candlelight, so over the past year, his room became candle central. It had taken him some time to light them all. Wait. This didn't look like he planned on dropping the hammer.

What was going on? In spite of how happy I'd been with him, my head went to worst case scenario at the first hint of anything outside of perfect. Maybe he wanted to tell me he got one of the jobs he'd interviewed for? Followed up with some extra-special saucy us time? *Please let that be it!*

He stopped and turned to me when we got to his bed. "Would you sit down with me?" He asked.

Weird. All formal and everything. He must feel bad about *something*. I sat down. My legs were shaky.

"I know we haven't talked about what happens after we both graduate," he started. "It kinda feels like we're both waiting for the other one to make some sort of move. Don't you think so?"

I nodded. "I haven't known what to say, or how to bring it up. I don't want you to feel held back, so I thought you might want to be free. I still have college, then there's another three to four years, depending on whether I go to law school or not, and you're at a different place." I stopped. I knew it wasn't going to be permanent, I always knew it. I had cheerfully ignored that fact during the past year. As Dhameer had warned, it was a mixed bag, getting what you wanted. I could feel the tears in my eyes starting to roll out onto my cheeks.

"What? What are you talking about? Why would I leave you? You think I would just date you while I was here, and then say *see ya*? C'mon Tibby, you know me better than that." He looked completely put out and almost mad.

"I just didn't want to be the reason why you didn't do something you wanted to," I said. Now the tears were sliding down my face. I couldn't help it.

"Baby, why would you think that? That's not it at

all. Here," he grabbed one of his shirts from a basket near the bed. "Stop crying. Please. *You* are part of the reason I am choosing the things I am. Why wouldn't you be? I love you."

I wasn't mopping up my face fast enough for him so he took the tee shirt and wiped my eyes and my cheeks.

"Would you please listen, without crying?"

I nodded. Tried to compose myself. This wasn't a break-up. It just felt so…great to not have the worst happen. I couldn't explain that to him though.

"You know I have been talking with the two different places," he said. I nodded again. "One of the things I have been trying to negotiate was where they would send me. I got them both to agree on the same places you narrowed down for your colleges. So depending on where you want to go, I'll have a job there. I want to be with you no matter what."

I couldn't stand it. I burst into tears.

"Wait! Why are you crying? This is a good thing, baby, not something to cry over."

"I'm not, not crying because I am sad," I got out, still crying. "I'm happy. I am so happy you would do this for me, for us."

"Why wouldn't I? I can't leave my wife to live on her own in some college town. Too many college guys for my peace of mind."

"Your what?" I asked. I was so surprised, and kind of in disbelief, that I stopped crying. Did he actually say—?

"My wife. Well, hopefully my wife. You know, if you'll have me," he said, giving me that smile of his. "Will you marry me? I know you're not even of legal drinking age yet, and I am totally a dirty old man, but

I love you. I want to spend the rest of my life with you. Marry me?" With that, he reached behind me and pulled a small box from underneath his pillow. He opened it, and offered it to me.

It was beautiful. I looked up at him, and he was looking at me with such love, and heat, and desire. I felt awash in everything I saw in his eyes. He was amazing. He was fiercely protective of me, kind of jealous about other men around me, which was hard as my best friend was a guy. It had taken a while for everyone to stop glaring. I was glad, because I had started to feel like the fire hydrant on the corner that everyone was trying to pee on. He was smart, and funny. If I married him, our house would be a disaster, because we both hated to clean. We liked completely different music, and our politics were not the same. But we had the same ideals and felt the same way about how to live life. I figured music and politics could lead to discussions that would keep things spicy.

Not that we needed a lot of help in that area. Sex was fantastic. He was very playful in bed. Having gone through a stage when I was in college in my old life where I slept with a lot of guys for all the wrong reasons, it was wonderful to be with someone who knew you and cared for you, who would laugh with you, even while naked in some truly awkward positions.

I knew this was right. I opened my mouth to say yes.

CHAPTER NINE

The glitter from the untimely appearance of Dhameer floated in the air around me as I realized I was in my bedroom. In my old apartment. It was morning. "God damn it all to hell!" I pounded on the bed. The room smelled like pee. *Oh, that's right*, I thought. *A giraffe peed in here.* It took too much to keep track of which reality I had fallen into. Not to mention I felt too depressed to care.

Dhameer was, once again, sitting on the corner of my bed.

"Are you kidding me? You drag me out NOW? After I'd been there a year, and he was *proposing*?"

"I told you, no promises of anything other than another chance. I explicitly told you that it was not permanent. More than that, you came to another crossroads. You had to make a decision that would alter your path, your destiny. You still have two more wishes before your fate is decided."

"What are you talking about? I want to marry him! Let me go back! And what day is it? My room stinks. How long has the pee been sitting here, stinking?" I was close to tears again, but these were tears of anger and frustration. I focused on the least important issue. Unless we were talking about my nose. How could he *not* smell that?

"You have two more wishes, two more times in your life to go back and do things over. Each will offer you choices. When you get to a significant crossroad, you'll come back. So that's three choices that will be available. Then, there is also the choice of staying here, in this life, now."

Figures. He ignores the part about the pee. "So I get to make the decision? I want to choose now!"

"No, not entirely. How that will come about, I don't know yet. And it's the day after you left. Basically, you have been asleep while you were getting your wish. As for the pee, I would guess since yesterday. I don't know. I don't do pee." He looked offended.

I sighed. Looked like I'd be cleaning the pee with no genie help. To hell with it. What did it matter at this point? "What about Rick? What's going on with him?"

"Unike you, he is waking up from a deep, dream-filled sleep. He won't really remember, although he will know it was a happy dream, and your face will pop up as he is thinking about it, but that's about it."

"What if I end up back with him?"

"Then life will go on with those choices you both made, and the lives you are living now will stop."

"Oh, god. What about his life? Is he married? Does he have kids?" I couldn't rip a dad from his kids.

"Anything in his life will be covered. That is to say, where he was will be filled with a positive replacement. If things are meant to be, and meant to have a second chance, then they are meant to be."

"That seems rather cruel." I couldn't get past the idea of kids.

Dhameer shrugged. "Fate is what it is. What is supposed to happen will happen, Toots. I was meant to come across you and offer you this. Where you are supposed to be, whether it be here or elsewhere, will become clear. I can't stop fate any more than you can. So onto the next order of business. You need to pick another crossroad and make your second wish."

My eyes filled with tears. "Can I have two days to think this one over? I'm still where you found me. I need to sort that out before I go and give some other life a try."

He actually looked sad for me. "I can do that. Two days. As much as I love to grant wishes, it pains me to see how getting what one wants can be so painful."

"Everything in life has some pain, right? At least, the things worth having in your life. I agreed to this, and I will stick to it. I just need a day to cry over Rick, and then another day to think about where I want to look at next. If I don't take this little bit of time, I won't give the next thing a fair chance." I hoped I sounded stronger than I felt. In truth it felt as though I clung to a cliff with one or two broken nails. I wished he'd leave.

"Very well. Two days from now, I'll come and see you, and we'll move forward." He was gone, leaving his glitter trail behind him.

Well. I stared at the place where he'd been. Felt the tears sliding down my face so fast that there was just a steady trail. *Oh, Rick. Were you remembering a proposal too?* I sat for a bit crying. This wasn't helping.

First order of business. Clean up the pee. I attacked the chore with gusto. Not just because the smell was getting to me, either. It kept me from thinking about all that had just happened. Once my room smelled ten times better, I got on the phone and called Xavier. Not only did I need to check in with him as my boss, spending the last year with him in high school like I had made me miss him.

"How are you feeling, Tib? Feel better?" How could he sound exactly the same?

"Actually, X, no. I'm worse. I went to the doctor. I have strep throat. It wasn't the flu, although I get some of the fun with that also."

"You don't sound so good. Strep hurts. Take the day off."

"Can I take the rest of the week off? I am really run down. I know it's a pain, but I won't be much good like this. I can barely get my ass out of bed."

"A week? I can't ever remember you asking for that much time off! What's going on? You must be sicker than you're 'fessing up to! What aren't you telling me? And how the hell is my empire supposed to survive without you?"

"No, really, it's just strep. You want my doctor's note?"

"Nah, I'm just teasing. Go ahead, have a week. It's better than me making you take time off to use your vacation time. Don't call me, just lay around and get well, and I'll talk to you next week."

"Thanks, X."

"Yeah, yeah. Rest up. I'll have a literal mountain waiting for your return."

"I have no doubt of that," I said, laughing and tossing a cough in for good measure. "I'll talk to you next week."

That was amazingly easy. Now I had a week to deal with whatever else came my way. I hated lying to my best—only—friend. I needed to ask Dhameer if I could have X in my life no matter what. He was part of my past, and I wanted him in my future. I didn't want to lose my oldest, truest friend.

First things first. I crawled back into my bed, pulled the comforter up to my face, and cried until the room was dark again.

CHAPTER TEN

Rick

Rick woke up in his bed, with the sun streaming into the room. He looked over for his wife and remembered she wasn't there. What was it he was dreaming of? He relaxed back into the pillow, thinking about what had been going on right before he woke up. It was nice, whatever it was. What was it? It was just out of reach. He thought over the details he could remember, trying to ferret out what it was that woke him with a pounding heart.

Tibby. That's what he had been dreaming about. Tibby. He hadn't thought of her in years. Why now? He crossed his arms behind his head. Tibby. What would have happened if she'd actually accepted his invitation? He wasn't sure that he could have let her get away. It had taken a long time to find someone else he liked as well as Tibby. He wondered what was she doing now?

Dhameer

He watched from overhead, hovering as he often did. He wasn't completely transparent, but humans didn't notice much of anything not dangled directly in front of them, so he was safe. He wasn't sure why he was so invested in this particular set of humans. They were no better nor worse than any others he'd granted wishes to. Well, perhaps slightly better. He smiled to himself.

He liked Tibby. She was spirited, and she had a sense of responsibility. It had taken her a while to find it, but she had it. He wanted her to find some manner of happiness. It's why he granted the additional wishes. He hoped it wouldn't turn out poorly.

Sometimes they did.

He didn't want to deal with the fallout, even though he had nothing to do with outcomes. He merely put the characters into play. Not that people who felt disappointed, or worse, cheated, let rational thought be their guide.

Tibby was different. She'd yelled at him, and he could understand that. But she'd composed herself quickly and just asked him to leave her be.

Every time he thought she'd do one thing, she did something unexpected.

He looked into her past. Ahhh. That was why. Her parents had been rather…unreliable. That would make a child more independent from an early age.

He checked in with the man, Rick, again. He was all right. Slightly bemused and lost in memory, but all right. That was good. He'd be able to tell Tibby, if she asked, that he'd seen the man, and he was fine.

He wasn't sure if that would help or hurt.

Tibby

That night, I cried myself to sleep. I slept like
the dead and felt like the dead when I woke up again.
I had taken my day to cry over Rick. It hurt like hell.
While I wasn't feeling as raw, it was still red and
painful, and it sucked. I hated that I was back here
and not with him.

The practical side of me looked at it as
needing to put the last year of my life in a box and set
it to the side. I needed to get through the next steps.
Knowing now that I would be yanked from wherever
I was when a crossroad was reached made me really
afraid to take any steps that would lead me to a
crossroad. But to hell with this. I'd let fear rule my life
for so long. I could see that, with my older eyes
looking over the past year of my life.

My parents weren't the demons I thought.
Not that they were great parents. Not at all. They
hovered around okay on a good day. But to have let
them decide my fate because of the fear they instilled
in me—pissed me off. At them. At me. I wasn't sure
how you were supposed to get over being raised in an
alcoholic family. You didn't know any better. I wasn't
sure I knew better now, but I had at least been
through the shit that not facing it brought on. I hadn't
expected to see something different from my
memories growing up when I did this. All my life, I'd
been aware of being the kid of drunks—and the
youngest to boot. It was a shitty place to be. It's why
Xavier and I were such good friends. He had a boozy
mom with a steady stream of boyfriends. He hated
calling anyone *uncle*.

God, I wanted to tell him about this. About
my realizations about my parents, although I didn't

know how to tell him without feeling disloyal. I didn't think looking back at his mom would show her in a softer light like it had my parents. But then, I could be wrong. Shit, how would I tell him about any of this?

One thing I had liked—he and I were still friends in my first wish. He actually liked Rick. Like my dad, X hadn't liked Dave either. I think that was when we were toying with the idea of dating, so there might have been more than just friendly concern in that dislike. But I had X still, which made me feel a little better. I hoped that would remain the case in the next two wishes.

I thought about this second wish. I didn't want it, if I was being honest. I wanted to go back to Rick, to marry him, and live that life. Dhameer had been clear. I had to go through with all three. I didn't think he'd just let me go back to the moment Rick had proposed. Why? Why couldn't I just stop now? This was a good place for me, and I'd be in a good place. A safe place. I could almost hear myself whining about how unfair it all was.

At the same time, I would never know where I was truly meant to be if I didn't give the second and third wishes my whole effort. So today, my think-it-over day, I mulled over where I would want to go, what I wanted to try to change next. After what I had just gone through, I hesitated to pick something that could be really great. I had to give myself a number of mental shakes to get me to focus and be fair to what or whoever was coming next. Even more importantly, I needed to be fair to me. How often did people get a chance to change their lives? This was a gift, and I needed to remember that. No matter how ungrateful I felt at the moment.

A thought hit me like lightening. How much of life had I missed by being afraid to face it? Holy shit. The thought was so big I had to practically shove it into a closet in my brain. But it made sense. Look at how afraid I was of potentially dealing with hurt again. I pictured myself shutting a closet door, leaving the lightning strike revelation and all that had been the past year on the other side.

It wasn't easy. Every time I thought about Rick, holding the ring box in his hand with everything he hoped for in his eyes, I burst into tears.

By the time I went to bed on that second night, I felt pretty sure I knew where I wanted to go next. I decided to sleep on it and see if it still felt right in the morning. When morning came, I awoke suddenly; completely awake. I thought about my second wish.

Yep. This was it. I took a deep breath. I was going to give this my all and tamp down any hurt that was still lingering. I hoped. As if on cue, Dhameer was on the edge of my bed again.

"Don't you worry about falling off?" I asked.

"Djinn do not fall." He looked at me with his slightly offended look. I was good at getting that out of him. I'm sure that garnered me lots of points.

"What have you decided?"

"Is this like before? I just think about it, and when it gets really detailed, I'll wake up in it?"

"Yes. I'll let you know when it's time to open your eyes as I did before. Are you ready?"

"I am. Give me sec." I breathed in deeply and exhaled. I did that a couple of more times. "Hey! I wanted to ask you something. Can I have Xavier in all three of my wishes?"

"What do you mean?"

"I don't want to lose my oldest friend. I love him. If he can't be in my wishes, I don't want them."

Dhameer looked at me so intently I wanted to squirm like a guilty kid caught stealing. What the hell was that about? It was an honest question.

"Were you friends with him at the time you wish to go to now?"

I nodded.

"Then you will still be friends. The only thing that initially changes is you take the choice you didn't before."

"Okay. Good. I can't lose him." I took some more deep breaths, then I looked at Dhameer, who was waiting calmly, and said, "Okay. Let's do this."

"Close your eyes and see where you are."

CHAPTER ELEVEN

I closed my eyes, and I was back in that tacky pizza parlor. I was visiting my girlfriend on a weekend from college, and Danni lived in Annapolis. I didn't often get weekends off. I had a scholarship for school, but I had to work to have money to live. My parents sent me money occasionally, but it was sporadic. They were proud and mad that I'd gone so far away. I'd saved for the outfit I was wearing that night. I'd taken forever with my hair.

"Open wide, Tootsie Pop," I heard the whisper in my head.

I opened my eyes, and I sat with Danni at the pizza joint. She loved this place, although I wasn't sure why. Tacky was kind way to describe it. We sat in a raised booth. I think the place had been something else in another life, and the current owners turned everything they could into space for tables, so we sat up on a stage.

A few tables away, a group of young men in white sat laughing and talking. Danni had told me about them before. They went to the Naval Academy. She loved mids. Her last two boyfriends had been mids. When she first called them that, I said, "Mids? What in the hell is that?"

"It's short for midshipmen."

"Ah. I'd look for a short nickname, too."

"Stop. They're really nice."

"And you're really a groupie. Only there's no good music."

I focused on where I was now, versus our past conversations. Danni, love her though I do, was tossing her hair and making goat eyes at the table of mids. I sighed. I had given up a weekend off with my boyfriend, Tim, to spend the weekend with Danni, and right out of the gate, she was on the hunt. So much for girl time. Although I had to be fair—now I'm glad she'd dragged me out. There'd be no second wish if she hadn't.

I'd been grumpy that night, though. I remember thinking that, but in reality, how much better was it that I was with Danni? She wasn't involved in screwing me over, as Tim was, probably right this minute. Danni was a really good friend (again, unlike Tim). She just hated being alone. I couldn't cast a ton of stones, because I had gone through my own stage of frantic coupling just to avoid being alone. It was a shit place to be. Danni was younger than I had been when I went down the path to stupid. It was hard enough as a sort-of-adult. At twenty, this was horrible. So I kept my sighs to myself and tried to be supportive without being mean.

The two other girls with us were her friends who had come with her for the weekend also. They were nice enough, but the whole lot of them were hair flippers. The mids were neither stupid nor slow. After a few more lingering glances and several hair flips, one approached our table.

"Hi," he said. "I'm Will. Would you mind if we joined you?"

"Not at all!" Chirped Danni. I think she might have batted her lashes at him. Good grief. I made a note not to bat mine. Admittedly, hers were a lot cuter than mine.

"Great," said Will. "I'll be right back." He hustled back to his table, and with amazing speed, he and his four friends were at our table, bringing over their pizza and drinks, and sitting down with a lot of chatter. Will and three of the guys sat down. His fourth friend looked around at the table, which was in a large half-moon booth, and walked away.

He returned carrying a chair from another table, and set it down at the outside of the table. He sat it rather close to me, as I was sitting on the outside edge of the booth.

"Hi," I said. "I'm Tibby."

He held out a hand, and I shook it. "Seth McKay," he said. "Thanks for letting us join you."

"We're practically the only people in here. No sense in sitting so far apart when it's much more cheerful to be with a big group." Hell. I did not sound twenty. I sounded grumptastic forty. Shake it off, Tib! I told myself.

He laughed. "Hey, don't go overboard with the enthusiasm. It could go to my head."

In spite of myself, I laughed. "Sorry. I sounded like an old lady. It wasn't meant that way."

"No worries," said Seth. "So are you from around here?"

"No. I go to school in Virginia. I'm just visiting Danni for the weekend. She's at school with me. This is where she's from, and her parents asked all of us to come down."

"Ah. A tourist. Good. I can practice my table crashing wiles on you and not have to worry about seeing you again."

I laughed again. He was pretty funny. I like it when people can make fun of themselves. It shows confidence. Seth had an easygoing manner, but he wasn't slow. I could tell he was capable and confident, but that he didn't feel he had anything to prove to anyone. I liked that. In spite of my sadness over losing Rick, I felt the thrill of attraction. He was handsome, and he wasn't shy about showing his interest. No games. He also had a very nice body. I needed to keep my thoughts above the waistline.

"Well, you're doing okay so far. I haven't run screaming."

"Not yet, fair maiden. Give me time," he said, arching a brow at me.

I laughed out loud. Everyone else at the table stopped talking to look at me.

Seth said, "It's me. She's captivated." His friends laughed and went back to talking with Danni and the other two girls.

"You're right," I said. "It's you. Entirely."

"It seems like there should be an 'Oh Seth!' or a 'You manly man!' in there, but I don't hear it." He gave me a frown.

"Are you always like this?" I asked. I remembered him as really funny, but now, I saw him for the gem he was. He was way ahead of his peers.

"Yes. If I wasn't, the pressure and my roommates," he nodded at the other guys, "would finish me off. It's only my sharp wit and wry sense of humor combined with my ability to insert sarcasm into everything that has stopped me from becoming homicidal."

"Well, I can see that you are barely containing the suffering. It's about to boil over, were it not for your heroic efforts."

"Indeed. It's good to see that you are getting a better picture of me. I was beginning to think you were lacking in the proper levels of appreciation."

"How could you think such a thing?" I held my hand to my heart, and looked wounded. "You came over to be merry and brought food and drink. Such assets are to be prized."

He looked at me for a minute and then burst out laughing. This time, when everyone else looked over conversation didn't stop like it had before. I caught a glimpse of Will's face. He thought Seth was weird, and apparently I was too. That made me like Seth even more.

"Where have you been all my life?" He asked, leaning onto the table and putting his chin in his hand. "Do tell. I'm mightily intrigued." I could feel the energy from him as he came closer to me. It radiated off him, like warmth. He was hot. Once again, why had I not taken the chance here? Oh, that's right. Tim. Tim the jerk. I stifled a sigh. Look at the amazing chances I kept missing for some guy who hadn't been worth it. I needed to focus.

"You're doing Shakespeare in Lit, aren't you?" I asked, flicking my glance from his. His was too intense for me with all the thoughts running around in my brain.

"No. I am naturally this worldly and well spoken."

I didn't answer, just rolled my eyes.

"I cannot show it here, for fear of being unmanly, but you have just sent a dagger through my heart."

"Oh, stop. I assure you, you'll live."

"I'm not so sure. Even now, I feel my life's blood fading from me."

I looked at him. "Does this work for you often?"

"Well, I'm not sure. I have to think about how many ladies have had the pleasure." He leaned forward onto his hand, pretending to think. "I would estimate the figure of potential victims at…one. So if you would be so kind, you'll let me know how it goes at the end of the evening."

I took a moment to study him. He was goofy in a way you would expect a goofy looking guy to behave. But Seth was not goofy looking. He was classically handsome. Straight nose. High cheekbones. Light green eyes. What looked like golden hair. I couldn't tell, because it was cut very short. It looked some shade of blonde. Not like Rick. Seth was only about nine or ten inches taller than I. Rick had been well over a foot taller. Rick was a mixture of black and white and American Indian. I could remember him telling me he was like a mixed batch cookie, sweet no matter where you bit. The thought made me flush, thinking of him in that manner.

I stopped my internal dialogue. This would lead nowhere but straight to hell. I had to close the door on Rick, on the last year of my life. *I'm sorry*, I said to his shade. I focused on Seth.

"I'll be sure to do so. I would hate for you to flog this as a good idea and strike out all over the place."

"Excellent. I welcome it. Would you care for a beer?" He reached for the pitcher he and his friends had brought over.

"No thanks. I'm not legal, and you don't get to tout your wares to the drunk girl."

He laughed. He had a really nice laugh. "So how old is not legal? Are you sixteen? Am I about to be arrested?"

"My not legal is twenty, so I think you're safe from the law. But you have more obstacles than that."

"Really? I love a good challenge." He flexed his fingers. "What am I facing?"

"A boyfriend."

CHAPTER TWELVE

"Always, always, the boyfriend pops up. Is he real, or is he a fictitious tool to send me packing? No, wait, don't answer that!" He held up his hand, and I shut up to see what would happen next. Even though I knew, I was enjoying this more than the first time around.

"Danni?" He asked. She stopped her conversation with Will, and turned to Seth.

"What?"

"Your friend Tibby, here. Is she single?"

"No, she has a boyfriend. His name is Tim."

"So he exists?"

"Well, yes. I thought I just said that?" She asked with a frown.

"Thank you. Carry on," he said to Will.

"I wasn't lying." I had to say it.

"Don't speak!" He held up a hand, covering his eyes with the other in mock dismay. "I am trying to retrieve all the pieces of my battered and broken heart. A curse on Tim. On all Tims!"

"Really, Seth. The school play must be right around the corner too. You're good."

He looked over at me. "I'm not entirely kidding, Tibby."

"How can you say that? We just met," I said. *Oh, Tib, you big fat liar.* You felt it right away, not just the first time, but this time. That whole instant connection thing, the love at first sight—this made you a believer all those years ago. I could feel my face flame again at my traitorous thoughts. I felt as though I should feel bad about where I was two days ago, but what I felt was the pull of my attraction to Seth. Not just a physical pull. There had been something more. There still was.

"More like we've just met again. I feel like I know you. What is Tim? Who is he? Does he know you like this? Would he banter in terrible Shakespearean knock off?"

"No, he's a bit more…sporty than literary."

"Jocks," Seth sniffed. "They smell. I should know. I'm one of them. You're lucky I showered, or you might be dead."

"What sport have you deigned to play?"

"Lacrosse. State sport, unofficially."

"I did not know that. Thank you. Another factoid to add to the Trivial Pursuit Cabinet of Knowledge."

"Happy to oblige, as always."

I smiled at him. I also felt like an ass. Why was I sticking up for Tim, who at this moment was attempting to cheat on me with someone I knew from school? I wouldn't discover this for several more months, long after I threw out Seth's number. Luckily for me, I knew Seth was not easily dissuaded.

"And with that idea, I must warn you. I plan to woo you from this Tim. He shall be dust at my feet."

"I'll give you an in if you'll talk normally."

"Done. What's your major?"

"History. Maybe a minor in German."

"I like smart girls."

"Me too," I said. "What's yours?"

"Pilot," he said. "I want to go into the Corps. Getting to flight school is the challenge."

"Ok, what is the Corps? And what year are you?"

"To you, I'm a junior. The Corps is the Marine Corps. As for flight school, by the beginning of next year, I should know if that's going to happen."

"That's exciting. You'll get to travel a lot."

"Not at first. Training is in Pensacola, and then you go from there. I'd like to go overseas."

"I don't blame you. Where?"

"England, Germany. Wherever I could get a spot."

"I have a good feeling. I think you're going to make it."

He looked down at his beer and took a drink. "I hope so. I think so too, but you never can tell. It's all I ever wanted to be."

"I envy that, the knowing precisely what you want to do. I'm not sure what I want to do. As far as I've gotten is that I love history, and I need to find a way to translate that into a career."

"That sounds sort of desperate. Why?"

"Oh, my dad likes history, appreciates it, loves reading it, but he's not so thrilled with the idea that I am going to have to work to find a job. He keeps pushing me to change it. So far, I'm winning, but he has two more years to wear me down." This was all technically true. I didn't want to spill all my family crap before I had to.

"Had you gone to an academy of some kind, your parents would have been so thrilled that you made it, they wouldn't have cared what your major was."

"I don't think I am cut out for the military. Too mouthy, as much as I admire the service."

"Makes me glad to hear that you could admire me."

"Who wouldn't? You seem fairly admirable."

"Admirable enough to cast off your Tim and see what else the world has to offer?"

"Would you respect me if I did that?"

"Why wouldn't I?" He looked genuinely puzzled.

"That I could break off a relationship over a chance meeting?"

"Well, normally no. But this is fate, or kismet, or something. There are always exceptions."

"You really think so?" As much as moving to the second wish had hurt, I was enjoying seeing things from a more mature point of view. It didn't change my mind about the essentials that I remembered; if anything, it solidified it. As with Rick, I was realizing why I passed this up. I couldn't truly appreciate Seth at twenty, just as I wouldn't have been able to deal with Rick at seventeen.

That said, to me anyway, that my internal meter of how I picked men was not wrong. It was just…not calibrated properly. I had good instincts, they were just beyond me when the opportunity was there, and then I ran round like a chicken trying to get something like what I passed up back into my life. It hadn't worked.

He leaned in a little closer to me. "I really think so. I think we met at this place for a reason. I haven't met anyone I've instantly liked the way I like you in a long time."

"Hmmm. You know, I didn't ask. Are you currently attached?"

"Had I met you three weeks ago, I would have to say yes. Now, thanks to my ex feeling there were more attractive fish in the sea, I can safely say no. You're getting interested, aren't you?" He smiled at me.

"You are fairly appealing, I will admit."

"I'm moving up the ladder."

"I hate to encourage you, but yes, you are. I just hesitate. I'm not so much of a love at first sight, or flash there's the one kind of girl."

"I could show you how to be," Seth said, looking right at me. "It would absolutely be my pleasure."

We were interrupted by the others who were dealing with the bills. Part of me felt relief at the interruption. Seth looking at me the way he did made me feel tingly. It wasn't just the physical with him. There was something about *him* that made me shiver. Once the bills were settled, Will looked over at Seth and said, "Man, we have to get back."

Seth looked at his watch. "Yeah we do. We're going to have to haul ass." He got up, and offered his hand to me.

Everyone gathered coats and purses, and moved outside. Danni and Will stood talking, while the rest chatted in a group. Seth stood next to me.

"You really should take the risk. It could be worth it."

"I don't like the feeling of disloyalty."

"Seth, come on, man we gotta go." One of the other guys had broken off from the group, worry evident on his face.

Seth looked at me, and I sort of smiled. He walked over to the car where the other four were piling in. I watched him go, and then walked towards Danni's car. I got into the front, and sat, not joining in the happy talk of the others. Danni and Will had exchanged numbers. I was so glad for her.

Here it was. I could feel myself turning red before anything even happened. And then, there was a knock on the window. It was Seth.

I opened the door. Why I had done that all those years ago, rather than roll down the window, I don't know. But I did. When I did, and had turned to face him, he leaned down, took my hand, and put his cover on my head.

"You know what this means, don't you? " He had a broad smile on his face.

I nodded. It was one of the many things Danni had told me in one of her *mids are wonderful* tirades. If they put their hats, their covers, on your head, you had to kiss them. I thought it was kind of cheesy, although it didn't feel all that cheesy now.

He leaned in closer to me, and lifted up my chin. He kissed me, softly at first, and then I kissed him back. The kiss went on. I didn't want it to end. Finally someone in the back seat cleared their throat. Seth stood up, brushed his hand across my face, and took back his cover. He put his hand out toward me, and I reached up for it. He handed me a piece of paper.

"If you change your mind," he said. He gave me one of the biggest smiles I have ever seen, then and now, and ran off. I closed the door, and just sat in the seat. I was astounded how amazing that felt. I won't lie, I've kissed a lot of boys, and had recently been kissing my love, but this thrilled me to the bone.

"Oh my god. That was amazing. Tib, what are you going to tell Tim?" Danni looked at me wide eyed.

"I'm not. I'm going to call him tomorrow and tell him it's over, that I think it's just not working out."

"Are you serious? Tim is a great guy!"

"He is, but I feel like he's cheating. It's been kind of bugging me. If I'm wrong, then I am, and he's a great guy. If I'm not, then I dodged a bullet." This was easy. Why had it been too hard to do this back then? I wanted to kick the former me.

"You can't just dump your boyfriend because some guy kissed you!"

"But Danni! He was a mid, and he took part in a time honored tradition!" I did my best to look affected.

"Shut up. He knew you have a boyfriend. Why did you let him kiss you like that?"

"Seriously, Danni? You really want to know why?"

"I really do." Boy, she was really bothered about this.

"Because I knew if I passed it up I'd be pissed at myself. And since I took the chance, I have to say it is the best kiss I have ever had in my life."

"Are you kidding me?" She looked surprised.

"Not at all. I've had some good kisses, too."
Oh, Rick, I thought. "This one blew them away."
What did that mean for me? I'd remembered that kiss
as the best one ever, but I hadn't expected it to be the
same after a year with Rick. To find that kissing Seth
like this was still the best kiss ever…this was getting
confusing really fast.

"I still think you should have told him no. But
if you really like him, you need to do what you think
is the best."

"Hey, if I am wrong about Tim, you're
welcome to him. Have at it."

"Wow. You really are going to break up with
him, aren't you?"

"First thing tomorrow."

Conversation moved to the happenings of the
others as the two girls in the back decided to join the
conversation. I sat silently, adding in only where I felt
I had to. I knew Danni wasn't happy with me, and I
didn't want to fan the flames and end up in a big
fight.

I went to bed thinking about Seth. I woke up
thinking about him. I felt as excited as I had the night
before. Since I needed to move this along, and show
my friend I wasn't a horrible person, I got up, not
wanting to waste any time. Danni had been short with
me after we'd gotten home last night. I didn't like it,
and didn't want it to go on any longer than necessary.

So I went to the phone and called Tim. He
lived in the dorms with a roommate, so I was
prepared for the roommate to possibly answer.

"Hello?" Said a sleepy voice.

"Hi, is Tim there?" I raised my eyebrows, even though the girl on the other end couldn't see me. She'd stayed over apparently. I didn't remember that from before. It wasn't a co-ed dorm. *Busted*, I thought.

"Um, he's not…he's not able to come to the phone right now. Can I take a message?"

Just as I suspected. I knew he'd cheated on me that weekend. I hadn't called him in the morning the last time, because I was too busy beating myself up for kissing Seth.

"Sure. Tell him his girlfriend, Tibby, called. As I am now his ex, you are free to spend the night when I'm on campus, not just when I'm gone." I heard her intake of breath, but before she could say anything, I hung up. I was certainly getting a chance to huff and puff on the phone and hang up on others in indignation in these wishes. That was kind of fun, I had to admit. She was in one of my classes, and I'd learned who she was at the end of the semester. I'd gone the whole time not knowing who she was. Not this time.

I pulled the piece of paper I had slept with out of my pajama pants. On it, Seth had written: *This is the room number. You'll get me or one of my roommates. Just ask for me. Take the risk.*

I smiled. I was going to take it. I dialed the number, and a garbled male voice answered. "H'loo?"

"May I speak to Seth, please?"

"Hng'n." I heard some mumbling and moving around, and then Seth was on the phone.

"Tibby?"

"How did you know?"

"Not even my mom calls this early."

"Seth?"

"Yes?"

"I changed my mind."

I heard him say "yes!" very quietly. Then he said, "Can you meet me downtown today? Let's have lunch. I can't get away until then, but after that, I'm all yours."

"I don't leave for school until tomorrow, and we don't have anything planned. Lunch sounds good. Where?"

"Middleton Tavern. I'll get a seat outside if it's warm."

"Okay. What time?"

"High noon. What else?"

I laughed. "You really are funny. I'll be there. I can't wait to see you." I smiled into the phone. It was true. I could barely sit still.

"I can't wait to see you either. Tibby?"

"Hmmm?"

"I am really glad you called me."

"Me too, Seth." I could hear his smile through the phone.

"I'll see you at lunch."

"Okay. Bye." I smiled again, and then slowly put down the phone. Since I didn't slam it down, I could hear Seth talking to his roommates. He sounded really cheerful. I hung up then. If my friends were sitting here wanting to laugh and be happy for me, I wouldn't want him to hear it.

Then I went upstairs to look through my bag and see what I was going to wear. Nothing looked right for the just-took-a-crazy-chance-first-date kind of way.

91

CHAPTER THIRTEEN

In the end, Danni loaned me some clothes as I couldn't declare anything date worthy. When I told her that some girl answered Tim's phone and gave me the whole 'he's indisposed' nonsense, she was outraged for me.

"That jerk. I can't believe he would do that."

"It really doesn't surprise me, Dan. I sort of had a feeling that something was going on. Now I can move on and not feel one bit of guilt for kissing Seth last night. It was not nearly what Tim was doing!" I laughed, I couldn't help it. I wish I had been able to see the girl's face or Tim's face when she told him. Even better, if she didn't know yet that he had a girlfriend.

Why did things never work out like this when you were young? I remembered the break up with Tim before. It was a couple of months after this, full of much drama and tears and many slammed doors. A lot of anguish for something that really was not the be-all and end-all of relationships. It did hurt me, though. Tim didn't help by telling me this was my fault, like him falling into bed with naked women was because I pushed him or something. Regardless, I was always really watchful with the guys I dated after that. Probably why they all became exes.

Danni was laughing with me, evidently thinking along the same lines I had been. "Can you imagine his face when she told him? I bet he didn't tell her about you, either!" She pealed with laughter.

"I was just thinking the same thing, Dan. His day is going to really be unpleasant today," I said. And we were both off and laughing again.

Danni inspected me before I left. "You look great. You really do. You don't look like someone who just caught her boyfriend cheating."

"That's because he doesn't really mean all that much in the big picture."

"Obviously," she said. "Jerk."

"Do I look okay? I'm nervous all of a sudden."

"You look great, I told you that. Now go, so you have time to find parking. Just walk down Main Street towards the water and you'll see Middleton's."

"Thanks for helping me get ready," I said. I gave her a hug.

"Of course! You have to promise to come back and give me all the details. I'm excited for you! Remember, ALL the details!"

"Yes, Ma'am," I said.

I drove kind of slowly, because I didn't really know my way around. Danni had given me pretty good directions, so I made it downtown and found some reasonable parking with no major incidents. I walked down towards the water as instructed and saw the tavern off to the left.

When I finally made my way past the thousands of crosswalks, I was right in front of Middleton's. Seth was waiting for me outside on the porch. When he saw me, he gave me a big grin, like the one he gave me after we kissed last night.

I have to be honest, I cried over Rick last night, quietly, so that no one heard me, and asked questions I wasn't able to answer, and part of me felt immensely guilty about this. I believed Dhameer though. He said Rick went back to his regularly scheduled life as well, so I really hadn't disrupted anything for anyone but me. However, the last time I had seen him, he was proposing.

Watching Seth look happy to see me, I resolved again to not let Rick be a part of this. Again. It was harder than it sounded. This all sounded fairly easy when I had been talking it over with Dhameer, but it was really hard while I was in the thick of it. My feelings were not so cut and dried.

I had a sudden major insight. Since the only person who was really and truly affected by this in the long run was me, if I didn't give each do-over the chance it deserved, I was cheating myself. I wouldn't have the full scope of what could have happened if I didn't give this my all. *I love you, Rick, but you need to take a time out for a while.* It was hard, but I envisioned myself shutting a door. I would leave the first do-over there until it was time to open the door and take a look again.

"You made it," Seth said.

"Did you think I was going to bail on you?"

"You never know. Nobody expects the Spanish Inquisition." He was completely serious as he said that, and took my hand.

I love Monty Python. "Our chief weapon is surprise, surprise and fear, fear and surprise." I didn't skip a beat.

"Not to mention ruthless efficiency and a near fanatical devotion to the Pope!" He came back quickly.

We both laughed, and I felt my nervousness ease a little. You had to love a fellow Monty Python fan.

"How can you scoff at fate and kismet?" He turned to speak briefly to the hostess. "Do you want to sit outside? We can, if it's not too cold for you."

"Outside would be good."

"Outside," he said to the hostess.

She led us to a small table in the corner next to the street. While you were practically in the street, it also allowed for great people watching. We sat down, and he immediately reached for my hands.

For a moment, we just looked at one another.

"So." I said.

"So, what's new with you?" He asked.

"Like you, I'm now single," I said.

"The dreaded Tim was vanquished on the strength of one kiss," he said, laughing a little. "Not so dreaded after all!"

"That is pretty much what did it. Although he dealt himself the final blow."

"How so? Did you see him? He lives around here?"

"No. He is still at school. I called him to let him know that I felt it just wasn't working out," I said.

"Why do you all use that line? Is it in the handbook?"

"Don't feel too sorry for him. I didn't even get to use it. Some girl answered the phone and gave me the hushed voice *he can't come to the phone* stuff, so I told her good luck, enjoy, and that she can now come over at any time. I really didn't have to do anything."

It occurred to me that in addition to opening myself up to two guys I had passed on previously, I had also rid myself of stupid boyfriends in a far more empowered manner than I had before. I had pretty much sniveled through this one before, just like I did with Dave. Now, I was putting them in their proper places, as they deserved. I wondered how that was going to play out. Dave and Tim were two of the several who hurt me, or broke trust with me, or generally made me feel like hell for things they did. They were also part of the baggage I toted around in my current lifetime. Maybe this was not just to find me my true love, or whatever I was supposed to be, but to show me how to be a stronger person and demand appropriate treatment from the people in my life. Specifically, the men in my life.

"What a foolish and sad little man." Seth shook his head.

"Why do you say that?"

"Why would he cheat on someone like you? I don't understand it. I practically threw myself in front of a train just to get you to call me. Sad, sad little man."

"Enough of Tim. He's the past." I leaned into him, smiling.

"Ancient history. But here we are, swirling in the waters of fate, waiting to see where we land."

"Dear lord. What are you reading that you keep slipping into Courtly Love 101?"

He laughed. "I am in a lit class that's studying Shakespeare, as you so astutely guessed. And horror!

Jane Austen! Way too many manners, although some of them are kind of appealing."

"It sounds like an intro Brit-lit class."

"It is. I'm squeezing in a few requirements that I sort of missed along the way. I want to get that all out of the way before next year."

"You can't hate it that much," I said. "It comes into nearly everything you say."

"Well, I am a natural idiot as well. This seems to fit with that."

"I think you're being too harsh. I wouldn't say idiot..."

"Really? Progress! What would you say?"

I tapped my finger on my mouth. "Entertaining?" Everything seemed bright and cheerful and full of possibility. All we were doing was sitting on a restaurant patio, but I felt at the edge of something big. Something more. Maybe it was all the Tibby-based insight I was gathering as I went along? I'd have to think about that later. I'd been right about him all those years ago. The potential was there, waiting for me to come along and take a chance with him.

"That is a spectacularly neutral comment."

"I'm taking things one step at a time."

"No whirlwind then?" He looked a little disappointed.

"I just told my boyfriend to hit the bricks after meeting you last night," I said. "What more do you want?"

"Oh, I want it all."

I looked—really looked—at him when he said that. His face was serious. Please whatever god may be above, don't count this as a crossroad! I want to be here longer. I waited for a moment, waiting to see if I would end up back in my bedroom or if I'd suddenly see a flash of the trademark Dhameer glitter. When it didn't happen, I breathed a sigh of relief.

"Sighs already? That usually doesn't happen until the third date. I'm losing my touch."

"Oh, no, no, it wasn't that at all." I didn't want to get into my issues "That's a pretty big statement based on less than three hours knowledge of someone." Maybe I could shift the focus away from me for a bit. Maybe that would keep Glitter Boy from popping in and ruining an upcoming perfect moment.

"I agree. What fun is life if you don't take a risk and see what's out there?"

Oooh. That was not so good. The swan song of the playboy. Time to get down to business here. *Be careful what you wish for*, huh?

"How so?" I asked, keeping my face neutral.

"Well, take the fact that we are sitting here together. Neither of us had any idea when we walked into that pizza place that we would be here, single, holding hands. I certainly didn't."

"Neither did I," I said.

"I took a chance in sitting next to you, and in continuing my pursuit of you even in the face of Tim, and again when I thought to stun you with my manly kisses. At any point, you could have shot me down."

"True."

"You took a chance in letting me kiss you. Cover aside, you didn't have to. I was just looking for a quick way to get a kiss out of you without getting all awkward."

"To stun me into insensibility?" I teased.

"If it worked, why not? You took another chance by ending things with the late, lamented Tim," he bowed his head.

"You are having way too much fun with him." I couldn't help but smile. It was funny.

"I'm the conquering hero. It is the appropriate time to bask in my glory."

"Shall I move over so I don't get in your way?"

"Only if you come sit next to me."

I leaned over and looked at his bench seat. It was a small one, like mine. "Seth, these are not two-butt seats."

"You could sit on my lap, little girl. I have candy."

I burst out laughing. "I bet you do. I just bet you do. Maybe save your candy for later?" I batted my eyes. And to think I'd been mocking Danni for doing this just last night! I switched gears so he didn't think I laughed at him. "I can't argue with that. So why did you take all those risks? Did I have *Sure Thing* tattooed on my forehead?"

"Just the opposite. It was more like *Not Available*. Makes it more challenging."

"All right. Fair assessment. Is this the way you tend to operate most of the time?"

"Not really. I take more calculated risks. I prefer to be more sure of the outcome. I didn't know if I was going to have any success trying to get a date with you, but I kept thinking, there is something special about this girl, and I will kick my own ass if I don't at least try."

"That's kind of funny. I thought the same thing. You're someone I would regret not giving a chance to."

He gave me one of those megawatt smiles. "Really? That makes me very happy to hear."

I had to laugh again. Seeing his smile made me so damn happy! "Let's stop this now before we analyze it till it screams for mercy. Tell me about where you're from."

He was from Maine. He was an only child. Pretty well adjusted for an only, which I knew was my large family bias coming into play. His whole family had been in either the Navy or the Marines, and everyone had wanted to see him go to the Academy.

"What if you didn't want to?" I asked.

"My dad and granddad both fly. I've been flying small planes since I was sixteen. Where else can you get to fly jets and blow your hair off as your daily job? The Academy was a smart choice for me."

"Um, maybe I'm an idiot, but wouldn't you go to into the Air Force for that? Isn't the Navy all about ships?"

He gave me a look of deep disdain. "How little you know! As if the Air Force has better pilots!" He sniffed, and glared over my head in mock indignation. All the while, his thumbs caressed my hand. It made it a little difficult to concentrate.

His parents were both IT people; his grandparents did something with shipping.

"I would think indoor professions were the best. Isn't it beyond cold in Maine?"

"It can be. We have a cabin up in northern Maine, up near the border, and it's like going back two hundred years when we go there. We have a well and no electricity."

"Please tell me you're not still using outhouses."

"We have one, but Dad found these composting toilets, and he moved the business indoors."

"Big fireplace?"

"Huge. But the cabin is small, so it warms up the whole house. I love to go up in the winter because it's even quieter than the summer."

"You won't get to be there much once you graduate."

"No, but it's where I'll go when I get out."

"Do you want to stay in for life?"

"Maybe. I don't know. If I get accepted to flight school, it's definitely a strong possibility. What about you? What do you want to be when you grow up?"

"Didn't I tell you last night? I don't know. I like the idea of law school. I'd also like to get paid to write, but that's even harder than law school to get going."

"What kind of law?"

"I am not sure. Family law, although that's really messy, or maybe maritime law."

"That's a pretty big gap."

"I know. That's why it's not a sure thing right now. I am also looking into working for museums. There are lots of avenues, in spite of what my dad says."

"Why? Doesn't he like your I love history major?"

"No. He calls it useless for making a living." I laughed. "I don't argue anymore. I let him rant at me, and then when I don't fight back, he throws up his hands and walks away. I wouldn't get anywhere anyway, so I don't waste my energy." Those were times I thanked myself for scoring a scholarship. If my dad had paid for college, he'd have cut me off. Of course, that's only if he stayed sober.

"Wise strategy." He smiled at me. "I still argue with my dad. Although, since I'm almost grown up in his eyes, he doesn't really yell at me anymore."

"I'm not sure when I'll hit that point with my dad. It's all right. He irritates me with his snotty attitude, but I know it's because he's worried." I laughed. "That's another reason I don't argue. He makes me so mad sometimes, I don't want to say the first thing that pops into my head." Why was I whitewashing all of this?

Maybe that qualified as a major insight as well. Maybe it wasn't so black and white with my parents. Maybe there was a middle ground. I focused on Seth again.

"Ah. Have a temper, huh?"

"Oh, yes. It's quick to flare, and then it fades just as quickly. I don't stay mad long."

"So Tim will be forgiven?" He had a sly expression on his face.

CHAPTER FOURTEEN

"I said I wouldn't be mad. Nothing in there about forgiving and forgetting. I won't even see him that much. He's a junior, and we aren't the same major." I shrugged. "Why do you ask?"

"Well, when you go back to school," He stopped, and looked away nervously, all slyness gone. "Are you going to forget about your weekend fling and run back to Timmy?"

"I don't think my now mandatory trip to the health clinic is a way for him to woo his way back into my good graces." I looked directly at Seth. He looked a little more hopeful.

"Good." I got to see the megawatt smile again. Then, with his nerves—and mine—settled, we moved onto other topics. I was fairly neutral as far as politics, meaning I disliked a lot of them on both sides. He was a mix. Socially pretty liberal, and fiscally conservative. I could live with that. He didn't seem extreme. He was more of a dog person, I liked cats better.

By the time our coffee was done, the waitress had been around several times to see if we were "okay" which really meant she wanted to drop the check.

I said, "Why don't we get out of here and walk? I feel like I am glued to the seat."

"I was planning to ply you with more food and drinkables. But your wish is my command." He caught the eye of the anxious waitress, and she all but ran over. I stifled a laugh. Having waited tables, I got it. Before I could even think about it, Seth had taken the check, tucked a card in the little sleeve, and handed it back to her.

"I think we kept her here after she planned to be gone," I said.

"She'll live," he said. "Can't she see this is the all-important first date?"

"That's kind of mean," I said. "Have you ever waited tables?"

"Indeed I have. My parents feel it's an excellent way to start in the working world. I started as a busboy, also known as kitchen indentured servant."

"I bet you rake in the money."

He looked at me with his head sort of tilted. "Why do you say that?"

"You're very witty. I know I would enjoy you as a waiter, obvious reasons and charms aside."

"Well, thank you. I was a smashing success. However, since the U.S. Navy owns me most of the summer, I don't work on my measly few weeks off."

"Really? What do you do all summer?"

"Go on cruises. It gives you an idea of where you might want to go when you graduate. This is my last year for one. Not sure where I'll be."

"Hmmm. Good to know."

"Is that bad?"

"No. It's good to know. I like to have the facts."

"I should know in a couple of months where I'll be. At least, I hope so."

Whatever I might have said next was interrupted by the waitress returning with the bill. Seth signed it quickly, and then tossed it on the table. He rose and took my hand.

"Thank you for a wonderful lunch. Company and food."

"Anytime, Tibby."

We smiled at one another while leaving Middleton's. "You want to walk down by the water?" He asked.

"Yes. Isn't that the touristy thing to do?"

"Absolutely."

"Then yes, let's walk to the water. I love being a tourist."

He looked at me, which was kind of a feat as we dodged the traffic in spite of being in a crosswalk. "Why?"

"Because you get to see all the best sort of things of a place. I also like to hit the dive restaurants and the pokey little shops, but I love the touristy stuff."

"Then I have a treat for you."

I raised a brow. "Do you now?"

"Indeed I do. Massive tourist attraction coming up."

"Lead me to it."

He smirked at me. "I like the way you say that."

"If I keep talking that way, do I get candy?"

"All the candy you want, little girl."

"You have a really bad side, don't you, Seth?" I couldn't help laughing a little.

"I can." Surprisingly, for what I had seen of him, he only smiled a bit, and didn't say anything more. That was…I don't know, sort of odd. It was a flash of something deeper. Another thing I would have missed at twenty. Was it good or bad? Was there a pile of shit behind all this attractive window dressing?

I made myself stop worrying. I'd find out. That was the point of the wish. To find out, for good or ill. And I knew I wasn't stuck here if it went bad. Not forever. So just go with it.

We held hands and walked in comfortable silence down the dock. There was a little canal where boats were moving lazily up and down to our left. It looked like the old cruising strips you saw from fifties movies, only on the water.

However, I wasn't comfortable, even if the silence was. His hand felt like holding one of those Fourth of July sparklers. You know it won't hurt, but it still puts off sparks that shock you. Seth felt *exactly* like that.

I started a little as I realized Seth had said something and was looking at me expectantly.

"I'm sorry, Seth, I was lost in thought. What did you ask?"

He looked at me with what seemed like concern, but said only, "I was asking if you're a water person."

"I am."

"Well, good. Here it is, in all its touristy glory." He waved a hand. We had reached the end of the dock and were standing in front of…well, a boat.

It wanted to be a New Orleans river boat. That's what the idea was. It didn't quite make it. Gave it a good try. It was super touristy. I loved it immediately.

"You have delivered on your promise."

"I thought you would like it. Let's get tickets."

We had a small scuffle at the ticket booth. I tried to pay for the tickets, but Seth wouldn't let me. I hate when people argue over a bill, so I conceded graciously, thanking him for treating me. He smiled at me, but didn't say anything.

There was still time before the boat left, but they let us on early. Seth led me to the upper deck. It was warm, with a little breeze. I was glad I had a jacket. It wasn't uncomfortable, though. We sat together on a bench towards the bow of the boat. He put his arm around my shoulders, and I scooted a little closer to him. It felt nice, very nice.

"You take all your dates here?"

"Only my mom," he said.

"Not sure how I can compare with that," I said teasingly.

"Mom is a high standard."

"As she should be."

"Glad to hear you appreciate mom." He smiled.

"I do. I love my mom, even though we fight like cats and dogs sometimes." Mostly because she won't stop drinking, leave Dad…oh, loads. I made a promise to myself to not go home if I could avoid it during this do-over.

He rolled his eyes with a great deal of exaggeration. "Women."

"Are wonderful," I said.

"Yes they are," he agreed. "Would you like something to drink?"

"Water would be good. Anything else would be too much."

"I'll go and grab us a couple of waters. Be right back," he said, and he headed for the stairs. I watched him as he disappeared below.

This felt different. With Rick, it was warm, and sweet, and comfortable. Of course, that wasn't entirely fair to Seth. I had known Rick for a couple of years before my do-over moment. With Seth, I was starting from scratch. In spite of that, there was something different. I don't know. I know I was paying a lot of attention to things he said because I was trying to see where the do-over might go. Poor guy, because I basically had an agenda. Thing was, he seemed like he was doing the same thing. Weird. Maybe this was a midshipman thing? I remembered Danni saying they were pretty focused. I gazed out over the water, wishing I was out on a sailboat, refusing to contemplate all these deep thoughts that would not get out my head when Seth returned.

In spite of the chill in the air, the sun had come out. I turned to look out over the rail at the harbor. Just being close to the water like this made me feel better.

"Hey," I said, turning to him. "Thank you." He handed me a bottle of water.

"No problem. I hope you're paying attention. I expect much wining and dining from you the next time we go out."

"I would love to do so."

"Glad to hear it. I have standards, you know."

"I should hope so."

"What were you thinking about so intently before I got back?"

"What do you mean?"

"You were lost in thought again, staring out over the water."

"Well, if you must know, I was thinking it was good wind today and it would be great for a sail."

His face brightened. "You sail?"

"Since I was little. I love it. Although I learned to sail on lakes, and that's a lot different than open water like this."

"I haven't done lake sailing."

"The winds are shifty, because the lakes where I sail are in valleys, and the wind whips around a lot more. I've capsized more boats than I care to remember."

"I'm on the Academy's sailing team."

"Really? That's awesome. I didn't know they had a sailing team."

He gave me a sort of snarky look. "Um, Naval Academy? Hello?"

"True. We have a team at school, but I don't race, so I don't really know which schools have teams and which ones don't. Smart ass."

"Why don't you race? It's fun."

"Just not my thing. I like to sail alone because I like the peace. And the being alone. Racing isn't really conducive to that."

We stopped talking to watch the boat push away from the dock. The deck hands literally pushed her away. She drifted for a moment, and then faster than I thought possible, the boat had turned and headed out towards more open water.

There were a couple of boats on mooring balls, bobbing slightly as we passed. I was struck at how many really nice boats people just let hang out on a mooring ball.

Seth didn't speak for a bit, then picked up our conversation where it had left off. "So no racing. Fair enough. You always sail alone?"

"Usually. I used to go out with my dad when I was younger, but learning to sail without him was like a rite of passage in my house." Before the drinking increased and nothing was fun anymore. Then sailing became an escape.

"How many brothers and sisters do you have?" He asked.

"God, a tribe. Four brothers and three sisters." All of whom I ought to call sometime.

"That is huge. Your parents are—" I cut him off.

"Insane. There's barely a year between each successive kid. My poor mom was pregnant for eight years."

"You want that many kids?"

"Oh, god, no! I don't even want to think about kids yet. I'm the youngest, I have four nieces and five nephews, and if I need a kid fix all I need to do is baby-sit."

"Nature's birth control."

"You know it. I also have a free-spirited sister and two very nature-oriented sisters-in-law, so I have been present for four home births. If all the kids in one place didn't cure me that certainly did."

Seth held up his hands. "I don't want to know."

"No, you don't. Suffice to say, I am not into kids. Not for a while. And certainly not a tribe, although I love all my family to death." As I spoke the words, I realized it was true. Good job, Dhameer. This was multifaceted.

"Did he teach you all to sail?"

"He tried. Not everyone was interested. My mom never has been, so my dad sails small boats. I wouldn't mind doing some long cruising, though. I think that would be fun."

Seth laughed. "You really don't know what you want to do, do you?"

"No. That must seem off to you, since you've basically planned out your life."

"A little. But not in a bad way. It sounds kind of fun, although I'd probably start to stress if I wasn't able to pick a direction."

"My mom says I can always come home and wait tables, if I need to. Only for a year, though."

"Why only a year?"

"It's necessity," I said. "With eight kids, you can't afford to have a lot of them loafing around at home after college. They need to be out on their own. My parents don't mind helping a little, but after that first year, you're on your own." All the others had escaped as soon as they could. Dad had been getting really bad by the time I was in high school.

"I can see why they had to make the rule. I wouldn't want any of them back." He laughed.

"Well, all but one of us got scholarships to college, so my parents got a pass on that. They don't like us being lazy, though, so that's why the one year rule."

"I like it." He hugged me.

"Yeah, they're good people." I couldn't help but to cast a quick glimpse skyward. I'd told so much fluffy bullshit about my parents I expected a lightning bolt at any moment.

"Except for this whole non-supporting the major thing," Seth said, teasing me.

"Yeah, and I can't really change it again. I'm in second semester, sophomore year. I don't really want to, but it's getting to the point where I can't. I'm already prepared," I held up my hands. "I can already hear Dad."

"You wish you could get a do-over?"

"What?" I whipped my head around to look at him. "What do you mean?" Why would he use that choice of words?

"You know, a do-over. Where you get to go back and make a better call."

"Doesn't everybody want do-overs about some things? About my major, no. I am content with it. I was in accounting because my dad and mom felt with my *affinity for numbers*," I did air quotes around the last three words, "it was an obvious choice. I hated it. So middle of last year, I switched."

"Okay, what would you do over, then?" There was an intense look on his face.

Wow. I was kind of caught off guard. I decided to answer honestly. It was just an innocent question. Right?

"Things I was too afraid to do, or try, or chances I wasn't ready to take, or that I couldn't see."

"Like what?" He persisted.

"You expect me to spill all the skeletons in my closet?" I asked.

"Sure. No better time than the present." He gave me a cheesy grin.

"You spill first, then."

Seth laughed. "Oh, no. I asked you first."

"We're out on this lovely boat, enjoying an almost sunny day, right? There you go. I took a chance. What else do you need?" I laughed at him, wanting to lighten things up a little.

"True," he answered me with a wide grin. "See what a good kiss can do?"

"Win, win," I said and leaned into him. Without looking at him, I asked, "What about you? What would you do over?"

"I guess that's fair," he said. "Probably being such a dumbass in high school. I was really lucky to get into the Academy. My freshman year of high school, I didn't take anything seriously. Caused me a lot of grief. My parents got to the point where I couldn't leave the house." He looked over at me, and rolled his eyes.

"Ah, you were a wild child."

A look of pain crossed his face so fast I wasn't sure I had really seen it. "I was. But I pulled myself together, and then sophomore year, my dad had me talk to one of his friends who was an Academy grad. It gave me something to focus on rather than seeing how much of my parents' liquor cabinet I could drink."

"Yours had one? Mine hid theirs. To this day, we don't know where they keep it. They said they had to, in order to be able to have a drink now and then." I couldn't believe I said that with a straight face. They had said that, but it was because they didn't want us to keep track of just how much they were drinking.

He gave me a small smile, and then as he continued, it was gone. "So I did get a do-over. Sort of. Some things, you can't do over. Now, though, when I see something I think is worth it, I'll take a chance. Calculated, of course, but still a chance. Life's too short." He looked off over the rail across the water. It framed his profile, and I felt my hormones give a very large twitch. He was really hot. And smart. And funny. And a Monty Python fan.

Part of the reason I'd wanted to see what happened with Seth was because I remembered how attractive he was. His looks were only part of it. He had a great many attractions.

So he had shit that made me pause? So what? We all did. I'd drive myself crazy over this if I kept on in this fashion.

Whoa. *Whoa.* It hit me suddenly—Rick, while a risk, wasn't really a risk. I knew, for the most part, who he was. In addition to how he felt. I didn't know jack about Seth. In that I faced real risk.

Probably why I insisted on going round and round over this. It was the second do-over, but the first real risk. I felt stunned at this realization.

My crazy inner talking lady made me smile. Just a little. At least this time she'd given me something substantial.

"What?" He asked.

He'd noticed the smile. "You really want to know?"

"Sure."

"I'm really enjoying myself. This has been a great day so far." Light. Keep it light, crazy lady. Risk isn't all bad, and this is supposed to be good.

"At least I'm still in the 'great' category." He looked amused. "I have a fighting chance of at least hitting 'okay' overall.'.

I smiled. He probably would hit the okay mark all the time. I tried to play it casual. "I think you do, too." I couldn't say that a lot of the things he said made warning bells go off for me. I wouldn't say it. It was my baggage, and no one else needed to share it, or be burdened with it.

"Well, good." He put his other arm around me and hugged me close. I let myself lean back into him. I thought I'd miss the tallness of Rick but again, Seth felt right.

"Tibby?"

"Hmm?"

His voice brought me from my own navel gazing. In my defense, it was rather important navel gazing.

"I'm really glad you called me this morning."

At that, I did face him. I wanted to see him. "Me, too. It was a smart choice on my part."

He met my stare. Didn't flinch. Looked right back at me, and I felt my insides go haywire. It wasn't just physical with him, although part was there. In spades.

"I have to agree. This has been really fun today."

"Even though all we did was talk?" I grinned again.

"Well, don't forget we've gone out on the premier tourist attraction!" He let go of me to wave an arm around.

I followed his hand with my eyes. It was beautiful. "I know you're kind of kidding, but I'm glad we did. Although it makes me miss the water fiercely."

"Me, too. Do you sail board?"

"No, I've never done that, although I've seen people. It looks like a lot of work! I'm not sure it's a good fit for my lazy ass!"

He laughed. "It is, depending on the wind. I have a couple of sail boards. Maybe we could go out sometime, and I'll show you how it's done."

I laughed. "Oh, will you? I just bet you will!"

He laughed with me, and then met my eyes. The laughter faded as we both fell, into one another.

Which sounds cheesy, but it isn't.

He changed the subject. "Since we have departed from the standard date M.O. can I do so even more and kiss you again?"

I turned to him. "I would really like that, Seth."

He had an arm around me, and he put his other hand up to my cheek. He leaned in, and kissed me. I reached up and put my arms around his neck, pulling him a little closer. He leaned into me, deepening the kiss. Oh boy. It was broad daylight, and I was making out in a public place. To hell with it. I wouldn't see any of these people again. I kissed him back with fervor. He held my face a little harder, the hand that was around my waist coming up to the other side of my face so that he was cupping it. Oh me oh my. I could feel my insides melting. He relaxed his hold on my face. I leaned back towards him and gave him one last kiss. I couldn't help it, it was so delicious kissing him.

"You are something," he said.

"That I am. So are you," I replied.

"I am glad you think so." He kept running his fingers through my hair. Occasionally, they would brush up against my scalp, and it made shivers run from my head all the way down to my toes.

"You have till forever to stop that," I said.

"Normally, I'd be all over that request, but I think we'll get kicked off the boat first," said Seth.

"Oh, wow. We're already back. I didn't even notice."

Seth didn't say anything, but stood and pulled me up with him. He held my hand as we left the upper deck and walked off the would-be riverboat.

As we walked back towards Main Street, we didn't speak. We were holding hands and occasionally one of us would look at the other, but not say anything. Being silent with someone is hard. When you find you can be comfortable and not feel the need to go on, not only is it nice, it's rare. I hadn't felt that before, at least not when I'd been able to stop myself, like I did today.

Suddenly, Seth stopped and turned towards me. "I don't want today to end," he said.

CHAPTER FIFTEEN

"I know. Neither do I." I found his honesty so refreshing. Why, oh why, did we play so many games?

"It doesn't have to. What would you like to do next?"

"What would you like to do? This is your town."

"Before I do anything else, let me call the guys and tell them I won't be back."

"You made plans for tonight? I'm hurt," I mock pouted.

"You never know how these things will turn out. C'mon, you know that."

I laughed. "I know, I'm just giving you a hard time. I have to call Danni. She'll either be thrilled or yell at me."

"She yells at you?"

"Privilege of being my good friend."

Seth didn't reply, he just looked at me and then walked a little ways away from me to make his call. I pulled out my cell phone and called Danni.

"Hey! Tib! How are things going?" She was practically screaming.

"Danni, calm down. Please. It's going well. I'm probably not going to make it out tonight."

She gave a whoop. "That is great news! You better be saving up the details, Chica! Hey, did you block Tim?"

"Yeah, why?"

"That explains why he called me, full of lies and crap. I told him you were out and I didn't know where you were. Then he said, 'I know she's there, put her on the phone.' I said, no, seriously, she is out for the day. He said, 'doing what?' I said, aren't you guys over? Don't think it's your business. Then I hung up."

"Danni, you are amazing. That jerk. You can block him too, if you want."

"Already done, sister. So, are you hanging out downtown? Will called me, and we're meeting down there later."

"I don't know what we're doing. We might see you. Don't stampede, please?"

"Promise. Okay, I have to figure out what to wear. Be good, sort of, and remember everything!"

"I will. I'll text when I am on my way back. Hey, you want me to text your mom too so I don't scare her if I come in without you?"

"Good idea. I'll send you her number and let her know. Later, girl.!" And with a click, she was off. She never lingered on the phone. I liked that about her.

I put my phone away and saw that Seth was still on the phone. He turned and saw that I was done and held up a finger. In a moment, he was done. He walked back towards me.

"Apparently Will and Danni have plans as well, in a large group setting," he said.

"She told me. Wanted to know if we'd run into them."

"I'd rather not. It gets pretty noisy in the bars here. Can you even get in?"

"I would rather not go to one anyway. So what's the plan?"

"I have an idea, but I need to make another call. Excuse me again," and he walked away.

I watched the boats still moving up and down in the canal. I liked this little downtown area. Danni always went on about her hometown, and I could see the charm. It looked like Seth had a couple of calls to make. Hopefully, it would involve somewhere indoors. It had been a little on the crisp side all afternoon, but as it got later, it was getting colder. My toes were starting to complain.

I stopped contemplating my toes as Seth came back over to me.

"Hey, is that a red nose I see?" He asked.

"Probably. It's starting to get chilly. Tell me we're going to head somewhere warmer."

"We are. I called my sponsors. They're out of town, but they don't care if I crash there when they're gone."

"What are your sponsors?"

"Families in the area who take you in during your first year. You can't drive or do a whole lot, and it's a demanding schedule, so they give you somewhere to go on the weekends to get you off base for a while. Mine are older with no kids, and they love having me around. Sarah and Jonathon. They live right down here, which has been great for me. I can walk or bike to their house. Easy getaway when I need it. It's warm, and they have a fireplace. Sound good?"

"I was sold on the inside and fireplace part. Sounds great."

"Let's go get your car. They have a place to park, and then we don't have to walk back later."

We headed for my car which was on one of the little narrow streets. Once we got to it, he asked if he could drive.

"Are you desperate for time in a car?"

"No, it's just easier than trying to direct you. I promise, I won't put a scratch on it."

"You had better not. I'll have your ass."

"Whoa. Calm down. I promise."

"You have no idea how much went into this Thing."

I have a 1973 Volkswagen Thing. I found it in a classified listing when I was fifteen. I begged my dad to get it and spent the year paying for it and for parts. He and two of my brothers and I had rebuilt the engine into something a little more beefy than the original. It took me two years to save up for the paint. While I was doing that, they built me a partial roll cage and bumpers, and then lifted it for me. I had added some diamond plate around the bottom and then put big tires and rims on it. Finally, my senior year of high school, I got it painted glossy lime green. It was beautiful. I was very protective of it.

"It looks like it. Did you do this?"

"I helped, although it was mostly my dad and brothers. I worked for three years to get everything I wanted on it. My mom did the interior as a graduation present for me."

"I'm not sure about the color, but I like the lift."

"I know. Makes it look more like a real car, doesn't it?"

"Should I just lie?"

"No, don't bother. People either love or hate Things. I love them. I accept that others are not as enlightened."

"If you say so," he said, taking the keys from me as he opened the passenger door for me. He shut the door and came around to the driver's side.

"Any special instructions? Wouldn't want to risk a beating over mistreating your flying lime."

"Show her some respect," I said. We both laughed. Love my car though I do, I know it's hard to take it seriously.

"Why does your plate say *Coconut*?" He was being careful as promised. I was glad I let him drive. I would have been lost. It was like a rat maze.

"Haven't you heard the song *Lime in the Coconut*? I know it's not that obscure."

Seth laughed. "You get better and better, Tibby."

I have to mention, I have that car to this day. I won't get rid of it. Every so often, my dad comes over and does an overhaul, and I still keep the lime paint and my coconut license plate. People often tell me that I should get a new car, but I figure, why? If the engine goes in this one, I'll just get a new engine. Thankfully, when I was drinking and partying a lot, my dad kept taking it from me. He always had a reason, fixing this or that, but really what he was doing was making sure I didn't smash it up in a random act of stupidity. I was mad as hell when he was doing it, but I am thankful that he did. It didn't jive with my bitter recollections of having parents who drank, but what I was realizing is that people all have layers. Some are good, some stink to high heaven. This was one of my dad's good layers. Or maybe he was trying to keep me from repeating history. Who knew?

It only took about five minutes before Seth was pulling up to a small driveway in front of a dark house off one of the million side streets. When we got to the door, he entered a code on the key pad. A light came on, and the door clicked as it unlocked.

CHAPTER SIXTEEN

The house was far more unassuming outside. Inside, the foyer opened up to a large open dining and living area, with a kitchen off to one side. In the back of the house was a wall of two-story windows looking out over the water.

"Wow. This is gorgeous."

"Yeah, I got lucky. They're right on Back Creek. They keep a boat here, so when they're home, they don't mind if I go out on it. They're really great."

"It's nice that they let you come here when they're gone."

"They know I won't trash the place. I don't have my friends over to party. Usually, I just come over to get a break."

"I'm very thankful. Okay, Seth, you promised a fireplace."

"I did. Let me get it started for you." He flicked a switch, and the fireplace turned on. I could feel the heat right away. I headed for the chairs that were in front of it. Even better, there was a blanket draped over each chair. I took off my shoes and curled up under a blanket.

Seth had gone to the kitchen while I was settling in.

"Would you like something to drink?"

"Something hot. Tea maybe?"

"I can do that." He moved around the kitchen and in what seemed like no time, came over and handed me a mug.

"What, are you still cold?"

"I am. But it's getting better."

"You could let me help you warm up," he said, waggling his eyebrows.

"I could. Pull up a chair."

He brought the second chair over closer to mine. He moved it right in front of me. When he sat, I put my legs across his and tossed him some of the blanket.

"Just met me and already sharing blankets."

"Aren't you a lucky man?"

"So far. You know, I can see that you've practically nested in there, but at some point, I will need to eat again."

"Then let me order us some Chinese. I love Chinese on nights like this." Maybe this way, I could actually pay for something. I didn't want him funding the entire day.

"It's a deal. It doesn't have to be immediately. I won't starve right away."

"Oh, good. I'm really comfortable." I wiggled my feet next to him.

Again with the comfortable silence. It sounds awkward, all these pauses. It wasn't. Seth was the first one to speak again.

"You never answered me before. Do you believe in second chances?"

"I'd like to. I like the idea. Don't you?"

"Only if you get to go back wiser than the first time around. Otherwise, you're the same person and you'll make the same choices, because all the things that influenced you the first time are still in play."

"Well, sure. Isn't that kind of the point? To go back and take a better path because now you know better?"

Seth took a moment before answering. "I guess it is. If you didn't have that knowledge, you'd be caught in a Groundhog Day kind of thing."

I giggled. "I love that movie. It would not be fun to be living that though. But even in the movie, he knew he was just repeating things. That's what made it so hard. He knew he was in what seemed like an endless loop. If you didn't know, you wouldn't be upset. You couldn't."

Seth shook his head. "Stop. It's like the never ending merry go round with you."

"I am very good at beating a point until it falls over and begs for release."

He laughed. "I can see that. So back to the question. You would believe in a second chance?"

"If it could be done, sure. Why are you so focused on this?"

He gave me what seemed like a very searching look. "Would you? Take the opportunity to do something over? I'll tell you, it's because I feel like I got one when you called me."

Wow, this hit close to home. I didn't want to lie, but I also didn't want to give away the farm in regards to all my *stuff*. "Yes, if the situation was right, I would like a second chance. I would have to feel like there was a reasonable chance that things would be positive. Not a guarantee, or anything, but at least a sporting chance."

He smiled. "A sporting chance. Veddy British of you, isn't it old gel?" He looked down his nose at me. Since I had read reams of Regency romance novels in my youth, it put me in the mind of a crusty old dowager. The thought made me laugh.

"Laughing at me already? I can see the downhill slope," he said.

"No, it's just…." I stopped, not sure whether to tell him what I had been thinking.

"Just what? It's okay, my ego is shattered, no need to try and buffer now."

I rolled my eyes at him. "I truly doubt anything is shattered, Seth. To ease your curiosity, I was thinking about when I used to read all those romances in high school, usually from nineteenth century England, and you looked like the old dowagers that seemed to be in every single one in them. It was the way you were looking down your nose at me," I finished, starting to laugh.

"God. And here I thought my ego couldn't be beaten down anymore. I was wrong," he said. "I am now comparable to old English ladies. What happens if I see you tomorrow? How much further can I go?"

"I don't know. You seem to be breaking records of all sorts. Wait and see. Maybe even you will be surprised."

"Not sure I can take it. Besides, I shouldn't have to. You're here with the cream of the crop of American universities."

I laughed again, this time even louder. Here was the mid attitude I remembered. "Is that what they tell you?"

He had the grace to look sheepish. "Sort of, along with why aren't we living up to our supposed potential?"

"Explains a lot," I said.

"It's not like it's a piece of cake to get in here!" Now he was looking sort of indignant. Dowager indignant. I muffled a laugh. He was right, it wasn't easy. I had learned that in the years after I had met him.

"I'm just teasing you. Calm down."

"You're not doing a thing to soothe my wounded pride," he said.

"Are you in theater regularly? You really need to be if you're not."

"I act a little, but nothing serious."

I smiled. "It fits you."

"You think so? I just look at it as something to do."

"In between what? Classes?"

"Yeah, and lacrosse. And training. And insane coaches. And study."

"What a busy life you lead."

"I do. I have to tell you honestly, I probably won't be able to see you as much as I would like to if we keep on seeing one another. I have to make grades to get into the aviation program. I have weekends, but that's about it."

"I appreciate your honesty, Seth." He looked at me funny. "No, really! I do! I would rather know that you have limits and are upfront about them. I can't really leave school during the week anyway. I have loads of homework, and we have a pretty big distance between us."

"That doesn't have to be a bad thing," he said quickly.

"No, I think it's actually a good thing. What about the summer?"

"I get about a month off."

"Oh, well, that's okay, then. I'll get to see you a little. You'll need to email and text, and let me know of your devotion in all other methods available to you, though."

"A little demanding, don't you think?"

I shrugged. No sense in pretending anything. I really didn't have anything to lose. "Maybe. I don't need you to be with me twenty-four/seven because I think everyone needs their space. I used to fight with Tim about it. Going to the same school, we didn't have a lot of chance to have our own space. But if we communicate regularly and keep the connection that way, I'm okay with that."

"I have to take that back. You're not as demanding as I thought. You don't know me. You trust me?"

Ah. The long distance trust conversation. Already. Wow. Well, in for a penny, in for a pound. "I don't have any reason not to. If you don't want to be involved, I trust that you'll alert me to that fact before you let anyone else know," I said with a smile. "I can deal with rejection, but I hate being the last to know."

"Fair enough. I'll let you know of my devotion daily."

We both laughed. "It's so nice that you're so accommodating," I said.

"What are you doing over the summer?"

"Danni wants me to come here and work with her over the summer. She always seems to make a lot of money from her summer jobs, so I'm thinking about it. What will you be doing?"

"I'll be on a cruise somewhere. Not here. But I get a month off, I can see you then."

"You do have family, don't you? They might want to see you. Besides, let's wait and see about summer. We may not be talking by then."

An odd look crossed his face. I wouldn't have noticed it, but it was striking in its intensity. It was gone as quickly as it was there. "I hope that's not the case. I, well…." His voice trailed off as he looked into the fire, seemingly not willing to look at me. Weird.

"You can tell me, or not. I don't want you to feel pressured."

He sighed. "I kind of feel like an ass. You told me you were involved with someone else, and I totally ignored it. I knew I had to make a move, but hitting on other guys' girlfriends is not my style. I feel bad, even though your ex sounds like a jerk. I don't feel too bad, though, because we're sitting here, and I can't think of anywhere else I would rather be. I just know my actions don't look all that good."

I shrugged again. "Tim was not my true love. I did love him, but the whole thing was dying. You can't take all the blame. I ignored my attachments as much as you did. He won't die, and you and I get to see if our initial impressions are right. Besides, Tim now gets a new, younger girlfriend and a cause to martyr himself over. Win all around."

He laughed. "How could you be comfortable for him to be with? It's a little unnerving, listening to your take on things."

"I don't know. I loved how different he was from me. But it didn't make us closer, or allow us to experience new things. It just caused problems. Hence his new and far more biddable replacement. What about you? You were recently involved."

He sighed, and looked away. "She wanted me to be there whenever she wanted or needed me to. Parties, weddings, since all our friends are getting engaged or married, whatever. I can't be there all the time. She didn't care about grades like I do, and I put a hell of a lot of time into studying. Plus, she wasn't real keen on all the moving we would have to do with me in the service."

"Then, like me, you're better off."

He took my hand. "That I am."

"Why don't we just see what happens? Let's try to get together a couple of weekends a month. You could come down and stay with me in the next couple of weeks if you wanted," I said. I wasn't sure I should have, it would imply all sex all the time, but I didn't know how much time I had, and I needed to see where this might have gone.

"I could next weekend, if you like. Is there somewhere I could stay?"

That was nice. He wasn't assuming he would be staying in my room. I liked that. "Uh, yeah. My room. We'll figure something out. I mean," I said, actually feeling myself blush, "Not like I am inviting you to an orgy, but that you won't have to sleep on the floor or anything." I didn't tell him I actually had an extra bed. I'll admit it. I wanted to see what he'd say.

"An orgy sounds wonderful, but I think maybe clothes ripping can be put off for a while."

Well done, Seth, I thought. You handled the whole sleeping bit well.

"Besides," he said cheerfully, "You have to parade me around as your latest boy toy and make the ex all angry and jealous. Since I'm sure I'm far better looking, he'll look like the ass he is, and you'll be lauded far and wide for your superior taste."

"You sure you're the better looking one?" I teased.

"Yep. Guys who screw around look like guys who screw around. I'm not one of them, so I automatically look better."

"Wow. That was very astute, Seth." I was surprised. He was far more mature than I had thought. It was a nice surprise.

"Since he'll be rubbing the floozy in your face, you need to fight fire with fire," he said.

I laughed. "A man after my own heart. You're willing to be used for such a purpose?"

"I would be delighted. I can be an ass with the best of them."

"It's a date then. Next weekend." He squeezed my hand, and I squeezed his back. By mutual unspoken consent, we moved away from relationship topics and into the finding out about one another.

We stayed in his sponsor's house all evening. He ordered way too much Chinese food for us, which he wouldn't let me pay for, and we stuffed ourselves in front of the TV. I resolved that I would get the bill first every time next weekend.

Eventually, I said, "I really do need to get back. Danni will be disappointed we didn't meet them out, and I was supposed to spend the weekend with her."

"I doubt she's even back yet. I know Will had his eye on her. He probably talked her into hanging out late as well."

I arched a brow at him. "The overwhelming charm you all possess?"

"Only those of us that are lucky," he said.

"Let me call her and see what's going on," I said. I got up, and he started picking up the remnants of the Chinese food massacre. I walked towards the doors to the deck, and dialed Danni's cell.

"Tib! Hey! Where are you?" I could tell she was in a bar, which made it surprising she even answered the phone.

"Seth and I are hanging out at his sponsors'. I wanted to see what you were doing. I feel bad, being gone all day, Dan."

"It's okay. Will called me, and we went to a late lunch, and then we came up to Harry Browne's. You should come up, the guy singing here is great."

"Um, okay. Let me talk to Seth. Maybe we'll meet you."

"Call me back! Bye!" She hung up quickly, which told me that Will was in the near vicinity.

"Everything okay?" Seth asked, coming to stand behind me.

"You were right," I said, turning towards him. "She and Will are out. They are up at Harry Browne's? Is that a bar?"

"Oh yeah, Seamus is playing there tonight. Yeah, it's a bar up on State Circle. Seamus Kennedy, he's great. He sings all the old Irish songs and a lot of other stuff. He's hilarious. You want to go over?"

CHAPTER SEVENTEEN

I was torn. Part of me wanted to soak him up like a sponge, keep him all to myself but that was not totally in character for who I was supposed to be at this point in time. Or who he was. So I probably needed to act more my supposed age, and go with that.

"Yeah, that sounds good. I have my fake ID with me, and it seems to work okay in the bars around here."

"That's good, they can be hard asses about it. If they don't accept it, we'll just come back over here, okay?"

"Okay, but we'll probably be fine. Tim got this for me, and it's me, with all my info, but it just makes me one year older."

He looked impressed, in spite of the mention of Tim's name. "How'd he do that?"

"We have a bunch of friends who are really good with computers and making things look real. C'mon, I go to a school where there are lots of really smart people."

"Well, great. Let's go have a drink and maybe I can get you to drink a little too much," he said with a leer.

"You think that's what you need? For me to have a little liquid relaxation?"

"Might make you a tad less perceptive to all my wily schemes," he said with a smile.

"Ha. You wish," I said.

"I do indeed."

I laughed. While he made the place presentable again, I went to the bathroom to see what I could do about the late in the day date look. I had some makeup with me, so was able to do a few repairs. It didn't really matter though. In looking in the mirror, what I noticed most was that I looked happy. I felt a pang for Rick and shoved it away. Time for that later.

I was happy. Being with Seth made me happy, but there was more to it.

I stopped the internal dialogue right there. I didn't do this in order to find something else to beat myself up over. I was learning. Learning was a good thing, as was learning from your mistakes. I left it there, fluffed my hair, and went out to find Seth.

"Hey, you look great," he said, meeting me in the foyer with my coat. "We can drive up there if you like. It's gotten pretty cold."

"Only if you drive again. I can't make sense of the streets around here!"

He laughed. "You're just trying to get me to drive the lime again, aren't you?"

I snuggled into him when he drew me close. "If you only knew how few people got to drive my lime, you'd be honored. Not making fun."

He held the door open for me and we walked to the car. He held the car door open as well, closing it carefully behind me. I loved how well-mannered he was.

Once he got in, I asked, "Do you go to this place a lot?"

He nodded. "We do. It's casual, and Seamus is funny, and the food and beer are good."

I took a breath before my next question. "Will you mind if I don't drink?"

He looked away from the road. "Is everything okay?"

"I still need to get back to Danni's, and that way, I can make sure you get home, too." There was no good way to say that all my fuck-ups came from times I drank, and I didn't want him to be one of them.

"Oh, well, okay. Great. Do you mind if I drink?"

"I met you drinking, Seth."

"I know, but just checking." He stopped as he maneuvered my car into a space on a tight traffic circle.

"No, but you ought to be aware that I will not carry your ass if you can't stand."

He gave me a scornful look as he got out of the car. I got out and he met me around the front. "I don't get that drunk."

"Okay. Then we're good."

He took my hand and led me to what I thought of as classic guy bar—all dark, with wood trim, and gold edging, heavy silver, and white tablecloths. Apparently there was also a restaurant on the main floor. He nodded at a waiter who was clearing off a table, and we went straight up a set of stairs just beyond the front door. Once on the second floor, I could see this was the bar area. It was lighter, not so much dark wood, but warm and comfortable.

No one was playing, although a guitar was propped next to a stool on a small stage.

"Seth!" Will stood up from a table on the other side of the room, and a chorus of greetings came from the people—mostly guys—sitting there. I spotted Danni sitting next to Will.

We made our way over. There were two open chairs across from them, and Danni gestured at them as we got closer.

"What have you been doing all day?" She asked, as Seth spoke with Will and a number of the other guys.

"Hanging out, eating too much, and talking."

"That's it?" Her voice came out as a hiss. "Good for you for the self-control! He's hot, Tib!"

"Shhh," I said, although I nodded. "I know."

She leaned in close to me so we could talk. "Will says he's never seen Seth like this, and that Seth is a little weird."

"I like weird. He's really nice, Dan."

"What do you think of Will?"

I looked up at him. He was still talking with Seth, and his face was animated and cheerful. He glanced down, first at Danni, then me, and smiled before returning to his conversation.

"He seems nice. He also seems to like you."

"I really like him." Danni giggled. "I have a good feeling about this." She said that a lot, but this time, I had to agree with her. I couldn't see someone like Seth being close friends with an asshole.

But what did I know? The little inner voice piped up. God, I hated that inner voice. It often seemed more snide than helpful.

Conversation came to a halt as the crowd began to cheer. A small dark haired man with a mustache and beard came out and picked up the guitar. I wasn't sure what to expect, but once he started playing, I was captivated.

There wasn't much time or room to talk with Seth. Seamus kept the crowd going, laughing and telling jokes in between singing. Seth got up to get another beer, and when he came back, he also brought a small glass of something dark

"Here. Try this."

"Not drinking, remember?"

"I'm sorry—I forgot the whole no drinking thing. This is the best scotch whiskey you'll ever have. Laphroaig. Some like it neat, but I like it on the rocks. I wanted to share." He pulled the glass over towards him.

I took the glass from in front of him and took a sip of it. Surprisingly, it was good. "You're right, it is good. Maybe another time."

He laughed over the music, and leaned in to whisper in my ear. "All part of the plan to get you liquored up. Too bad you're on to me. What sucks even more is how sexy you look drinking my whiskey and I can't do anything about it."

I laughed and snuggled into him. He felt fantastic. The whiskey was a warmth that went through me even with one little sip.

All too soon, he was done for the night. Seth turned to me.

"So, do you have to go?"

I didn't want to, but I nodded. "I do. I really need to get some sleep. We have to drive back to school tomorrow." I looked over at Danni. She and

Will were sitting with their heads close together, talking.

"Can I meet you for brunch tomorrow before you go?"

"Hang on." I leaned across the table and got Danni's attention. "Hey! Come up for air!"

She looked at me and dismissively waved a hand. "What?"

"What time are we leaving tomorrow?"

"I don't know. One or two, maybe?"

"Great. Then Will I would love to take you ladies to brunch," Seth interrupted. "Wouldn't we, Will?"

Will nodded, and met Danni's eye. "Would you like to?"

"When and where?" Danni asked the two of them with a laugh.

"Carrol's Creek. Eleven. It's the best brunch around," Seth said immediately. I felt like perhaps he'd had this in mind before now.

"We're there. But we should be getting back, Tib."

Neither Danni nor I really wanted to leave. It didn't do to look too eager, so we all stood, getting our coats and stuff together.

"Can I ride home with you?" Danni asked. That was odd. Normally, she'd want to be with Will, but...

"Sure. Um, I need to take Seth back," I said.

Will solved that problem for me. "We can walk back, Tibby. The gate's close to here."

I turned to Danni. "Can you get me out of here? This place is crazy."

She laughed and nodded, and we made our way downstairs. Out front, the troop of guys that had been sitting at our table moved up the sidewalk, stopping at the corner. They were waiting for Will and Seth.

Seth gathered me close. "I had a great time today. I can't wait to see you tomorrow." He leaned down and his lips were on mine. I could taste the beer and the whiskey on him. It tasted great.

Oh my lord. As before, my entire body felt like it was going up in flames. The boy could kiss! I wrapped my arms around him and kissed him back enthusiastically.

Suddenly, he let me go. "It's hard to keep myself under control with you." His voice was hoarse.

I got it. "Well, good thing we both have a veneer of civilization," I tried to lighten the moment. If we'd been alone, I couldn't guarantee I would have stopped then. In spite of all my concerns and warnings to myself. I got the impression he was struggling with the same kind of feelings.

"C'mon Seth," Will called. Apparently he and Danni had already said their good-byes. She was smiling at us, and with a last peck on the lips, Seth smiled that wonderful smile at me and loped off to join Will and the other guys. They turned the corner in a herd, a cheerful mutter coming from them.

Danni threaded her arm through mine. "Well, c'mon. Let's go. You have a lot to spill."

"And you don't?" I asked. "You look really happy."

She was glowing. "He is really nice, and he's not a jerk. He didn't kiss me like you two were kissing!" Was that condemnation I heard in her voice?

"It's weird. I don't normally get all physical with a guy when we first meet, but I can't seem to stop wanting to kiss him," I confessed, hoping to soften condemnation if there was any.

"No, you usually don't. Is this like a rebound or something?"

Shit. I'd forgotten totally about Tim. Not hard as to me, he was six years in the past. But to Danni, I'd broken up with him this morning. No wonder she thought this was a rebound.

I had another flash of insight. That was when I started fooling around with guys a lot and being kind of slutty. After Tim broke my heart and did a major mind fuck on me. Before that, I had a lot of barriers. The hurt I let him cause me also led me to drop nearly all of them. If I recalled correctly, that was when Danni and I had stopped being such good friends. I'd slept with, on a whim, a guy one of her friends liked and was sort of dating. It had been the last straw.

I hadn't known about the friend, but that didn't matter. She'd been concerned over my behavior since Tim and I broke up.

I squeezed her hand. "I know it seems sudden, but I should have ended it with Tim a while ago. Even without the fact that he was cheating," I said. "We were just growing apart, and I didn't realize it. When I met Seth, I suddenly saw all the things that were missing with Tim. And then my suspicions recently."

"Why didn't you tell me? I could have done a little detective work for you," Danni said as we got into my car.

"I didn't want to think about it. It felt really embarrassing to think that he was fooling around."

She leaned over and gave me a one-armed hug. "It's not your fault that you trusted him! That's what you're supposed to do."

"I know, but I still feel stupid."

"Well, you're not. He's a jerk. But you don't think Seth is just a rebound kind of thing?"

I shook my head, turning up the heater. "No. He's special. I could feel it when I met him. Spending the day with him today just reinforced that, you know?"

"I'm glad for you, Tibby. I really am. I'm still stuck on the fact that Tim was actually cheating. He seemed like such a nice guy!" She shook her head in wonder.

"He was. I'm betting this wasn't the first time. I don't know why he had to cheat. All he had to do was break up with me. I think he liked the thrill." I didn't think that, I knew it. He'd screamed it at me when we were fighting in my other life. That Ms. Thing had been exciting, and willing to do new things, unlike boring-ass old me.

The thought made my blood boil. I took a deep breath, because now, that wasn't going to be my future. Even if I didn't stay here, I was changing. That would change my life regardless of where I was.

"I'm glad you know now, rather than letting this go on. Oh my god!" Her hand flew to her mouth.

"What?" I resisted the urge to slam on the brakes.

"You need to go get tested, Tib! Who knows what he's been sleeping with?"

"Oh, I planned on it."

"Enough about that asshole. Tell me all about Seth."

Where did I start? I talked the rest of the ride home, trying to tell her things that didn't give me away as a different Tibby, things I knew she'd enjoy hearing. Like his sense of humor, the nice place that we hung out in, the fact that he was coming down to Tech next weekend.

"What? He's already coming to see you? Where is he going to sleep?" Danni always got to the pertinent issues.

"He can stay with me, but we're not sleeping together. Don't get me wrong, it's gonna be really hard. I mean, look at him! He's gorgeous, and he's got that smile, he's funny, and nice, I laugh with him, and he can kiss like crazy…" My voice trailed off as I realized I was smiling thinking about all these aspects of Seth.

Danni laughed. "Girl, you have it bad! But I'm happy for you. This way, you're not moping or wondering what you did wrong with loser. Much better this way."

Amazing how she picked up on exactly what I did do the last time around. "I feel good, Dan. Like this is the way I'm supposed to be going."

"No, it's not, honey."

"What?"

"You need to turn around. We went the wrong way."

We both burst into laughter. We'd been so busy talking that she'd forgotten to tell me when to turn, and I'd forgotten to ask.

We made it back to her house, and tried to come in quietly. Thankfully, her parents were asleep or pretending to be.

"I still don't have anything to wear tomorrow," I said, as we got into bed.

"Just wear what you're comfortable in. I've seen how he looks at you. He won't care if you're dancing around in a paper bag."

"He'd probably like it," I said darkly, imagining how he could tear such a thing right off me.

That sent us off into peals of laughter, and we finally smothered it and settled in.

I couldn't wait for tomorrow.

Three Wishes

CHAPTER EIGHTEEN

The next morning, we both raced around trying to get ready. Danni's mom, hearing where the guys wanted to eat, had been impressed. "They must like you. That's a nice place for a second date."

"Yes, but is the food good?" Danni asked her mom.

"Yes, it is. You'll like it," she smiled at her daughter. "It's one of the nicer brunches around."

That just put the pressure on more, and we barely made it out of the house in time to get there. This time, Danni drove my car, as she knew the way. She also had the proper respect for my girl. We pulled into the parking lot.

"I don't see them," I said.

"They won't stand us up," she replied. "They're probably inside."

They weren't. As soon as we got of the car, they both emerged from a car a few rows over from us.

Seth greeted me with a big hug. I couldn't see how Will and Danni said hello, but I could hear the tone in her voice behind me. She was happy.

"Let's go! I'm starving," Seth said, keeping an arm around me.

Danni's mom had been right. The food was amazing, and like yesterday, I ate more than I should have.

During brunch, I watched Will. I wanted him to be nice to Danni. If he wasn't going to be a keeper, I wanted him to be nice while he was with her. What I saw was that he liked her, although he wasn't as open as Seth. Seth actually sat next to me and held my hand under the table most of the meal.

I could tell Danni really liked Will, too. I sent a silent plea out into the universe for Danni to not get hurt. Knowing what I did about her, and what I knew now, she needed a nice guy. For all her confidence, she hid a massive amount of insecurity.

All too soon, we were finished with the meal.

The guys paid, and we were all outside again. I didn't want this to end.

"I'll see you next weekend," Seth said into my ear. Like when we'd met, he took me in his arms and wrapped me up again. I felt safe and cared for.

"Absolutely. I can't wait to see you," I said.

He leaned down and kissed me. Maybe he was feeling shy, maybe it was because we were in broad daylight, but it wasn't the socks-falling-off passionate kiss from last night.

Not that I was complaining! It was different, full of care and concern.

"A week is going to seem too long," he whispered. "Call me when you get home, okay? So I know you made it?"

"Okay."

"And so I can practice my wiles on you a little more," he added. That brief flash of insecurity moved across his face. I wasn't sure if I'd actually seen it, because his eyes were warm as he looked at me.

Danni and I got into my car, and I waved as we pulled out of the parking lot. He and Will stood there until we turned the corner and couldn't see them.

I sighed and leaned back in the seat.

"I know. They are both just awesome, aren't they?" Danni asked. Her face had a dreamy expression.

"Yes. I'm so glad you asked me to come home with you."

"You mean forced you? And who wouldn't be, meeting someone like Seth?" Danni's tone was teasing.

"That's part of it. But if I had stayed home, I wouldn't have known about Tim, for who knows how long. I wouldn't have gotten to hang out with you, my bestie, and if I wasn't with you, I'm not sure I would have had the courage to dump Tim." I smiled at her. I didn't want her to think I was only glad for the guy factor. I also wanted to make sure I didn't lose her as a friend again. I wanted her to know what I thought of her.

Danni's face softened. "I'm glad you're here, too. It's been a great weekend, hasn't it?"

I nodded, and we didn't talk on the rest of the ride home, both lost in our thoughts. Once we got back to her parents' place, I packed up and left. Danni would be leaving a little later. She'd asked me to drive along with her, but I needed the time to think. Everything had happened so fast.

I was still here, so obviously, I hadn't hit the next big crossroads. But unlike Rick, where things stretched out for over a year, this was going from zero to one hundred in the course of a weekend. Even with all my insights into myself, and my behavior, and the way things went in my future—my past future—I still hadn't been pulled out by Dhameer.

I honestly felt afraid of when that would happen. The pain of being taken from wish number one when Rick had proposed was still very much there. Only sheer force of will and the desire to not cheat myself, in spite of the tears my heart cried, kept me from curling up into a ball.

I laughed a little. I kept telling myself that, but the pain of leaving Rick wasn't really easing. What would have happened had I gotten engaged just as I was getting ready to go to college? Would we have made it?

He'd planned for us to be in the same town, so I have to think that we would have. That means by now, I'd have married him—I mean, if I'd stayed in that wish and been twenty-six. We might even be having kids.

The thought of our non-existent kids made tears spring to my eyes. I had meant it when I told Seth that I didn't want any, but there was something intoxicating about the thought of having kids with someone you loved.

I was halfway home before the tears stopped. Okay. I needed to focus on Seth. What happened next?

I had to keep telling myself it didn't matter— that I wouldn't be staying here, so now wasn't the time for hesitation.

When I walked into my room, I realized I had more immediate problems. If I didn't clean this place up, he'd take one look and run screaming.

Three weeks later

I was really excited to see him. The first weekend had been great. I had managed to keep my libido under control, and he had been a perfect gentleman. He had squired me around, met some of my friends, and basically just spent time in my life. It had been wonderful. We had talked on the phone every night for the past two weeks, and I found that today I impatiently waited for him to get here. I was excited to see him, to touch him, and to see if things were still as I felt they were. The ache from Rick hadn't dissipated, but Seth eased it. Unlike Rick, things were still going a million miles an hour. I was afraid to admit it to myself for fear of vanishing in a cloud of glitter, but I was on my way to being in love. I could barely think the words, but they were there. *Oh, please, please leave me here longer!* I sent out a silent plea.

While I was musing over this in my head, there was a loud knock at the door. I leapt from my seat and almost ran to answer it. When I opened it, he was there. He dropped his bag and gathered me into a huge embrace. We stood together for a moment, and I felt like I had come home. How did he get to this place with me so fast?

"Why don't you come in?" I said.

"What, and stop the show for your neighbors? Spoilsport," he said.

"I have nothing against exhibitionism, but I feel more comfortable without it."

"Pity. Here I thought you were adventuresome."

"Oh, no. None of that guilt thing here. Did you ever think I wasn't interested in sharing any aspect of you with anyone else?" I teased.

"Oh, well that would be fine. I am completely okay with you being all possessive and selfish," he said. He came into my little room, filling it up as he'd done before.

"You made good time getting here," I said, feeling a little breathless. He did that, overwhelmed me at times.

"I had a good reason to hurry." He leaned down to kiss me. This might be the weekend that we ended up naked. The thought excited and unnerved me. You got to see a lot more than just naked ass the first time you took your clothes off in front of someone else. The first weekend he'd visited, there was a little dancing around one another, both of us being careful. But he kissed me, a lot, and I could tell he was struggling with his desire also. It didn't help that the more we talked, and got to know one another, the more I knew he could be the right one. How do you choose between two Mr. Rights?

I also had the problem of nearly a month with no sex when I'd been having it regularly. It was hard going from gourmet-all-you-can-eat to nothing and the cupboard is bare! To say I was frustrated would be an understatement.

I didn't want to rush this, though. Partly because I wanted to do this right, and selfishly, because I wasn't ready to go back to my old life, where giraffe pee was the most exciting thing in my apartment in ages.

"What are we doing for dinner?" Seth asked. That sounded so domestic.

"I don't know, I hadn't thought about it. You want to go downtown? There's a bar that does great burgers."

"And you can get in?" We hadn't gone out much at night when he'd been here last. We'd ordered in and watched movies, and cuddled and kissed and touched. He'd slept in the other bed in the room, since I didn't have a roommate. My former roommate had dropped out, and the school hadn't gotten around to assigning me a new one. I was fine with it. I liked being able to have a room to myself. Particularly now. If things kept heating up, I'd never want a roommate again.

"Fake ID, remember?"

"Oh, that's right. I forgot. Great. Let's go. I'm starving."

I drove us down to the T. It was still early, by college standards, so we got a table easily.

"Oh my god," I said. Shit. I couldn't catch a break here.

"What?" Seth asked.

"Tim is here."

"Good." He reached across the table, and pulled my hand over, bringing it to his lips. He kissed it, and then made eye contact with me. "Don't even look around. Don't pay him any mind at all. Trust me."

I smiled and allowed myself to relax. Who cared if Tim was here? I'd avoided seeing him since I'd met Seth. He would have moved along by now. As long as he wasn't as assy as he'd been before. Seriously, though. With thousands of students, why did I have to run into him tonight?

Not that Seth looked bothered. In fact he looked like the head rooster in the henhouse. I'm not sure he could have puffed up any more.

"I'm glad you still let me come visit, Tibby."

"Why wouldn't I?" This changed my train of thought immediately.

Seth shrugged. "Sometimes, the newness fades really fast." Why did his voice sound so sad? Was this part of his mysterious past?

"You know, you're going to have to actually explain all these cryptic comments one day," I said, tickling his hand with my fingers.

"I will. You'll have to do the same."

"You want a big share fest?" I smiled to show him I was teasing.

"No, not really. But it's probably the right thing to do." Oh. Now I definitely heard something.

"Let's table it, okay?"

At that moment, the waitress came over. I was glad for the interruption. I didn't want to get into anything serious. That might constitute a crossroad, and I wasn't ready to leave yet. I had a feeling that I wasn't going to get as long as I had with Rick. Rick had been a more regular part of my life, so it took more for me to reach a crossroads. Seth was shiny and new, and I felt like something was coming. Unlike Seth, I didn't worry about the newness fading. It kept getting better and better. I didn't think it possible, but it did.

I just wasn't sure what. I didn't want to leave this either. *There's that catch again, right Dhameer? I* thought. *Get what you want, and when you get it, it's not exactly what you want. But you get it. Every bit of it.*

I couldn't dispel my thoughts of what I figured was coming later. It had that feel. The anticipation. All our glances, our touches—our everything—were supercharged. It'd been some time since I felt this way with someone. The newness. No booze to cloud things. The excitement, both of us in a relatively good place. In and of itself, that newness was intoxicating.

Oh, god, I hoped we had sex. I don't think I could stand to see him without his shirt and not stroke his abs one more night. What would sex be like with him? Someone who cared about me? A lot? Someone I felt the same way about? Someone who—

"Tib?"

"Oh, I'm sorry!" I saw that both Seth and the waitress were waiting on me to order something. "Can I just have a Coke?"

She nodded, smiled at Seth again, and hurried away. Uh huh. He was hot, but the waitress needed to mind her manners. I glared in the direction she'd gone.

Which put me right in the crosshairs of Tim. Damn it.

He took that to mean I wanted to talk to him, or something of the sort, because he stood and headed our way.

"Asshole alert," I said to Seth quietly. "He's coming towards us."

Seth shrugged. "Let him. He's already lost."

I squeezed his hand across the table. I could fall in love with this guy. Honestly. He was just so fucking awesome.

"Tibby."

Oh for fuck's sake. Did he always sound so pompous? Probably. I just wasn't able to see it back then. For some reason, I felt lucky he wanted to date me.

"Tim." I felt Seth tense, and I patted his hand. I wanted him to know I had this.

"What are you doing here?"

I looked around in exaggerated surprise. "Why, the same as everyone else. Out with my guy, getting something to eat before we head home for the night." I smiled brightly, and Seth gave me one of the megawatts. If we did have sex, he was getting something special in his stocking. For sure.

"Just as I thought. A total slut. Well, enjoy my leftovers, sucker." He went to clap Seth on the shoulder, but Seth whipped around and grabbed his hand.

"You must be the dumbass."

Tim's eyes actually bugged. I'd always thought it was just an expression, but they actually bugged out. It was hilarious, and I wanted to giggle.

"What did you call me?"

"The dumbass. The dumbass who was fucking someone else when you had this girl. You lose, sucker. I win. Now get the hell out of here." At that point, Seth stood up, still gripping Tim's hand. He twisted it a little, and I saw Tim wince. Then Seth let go, and clapped Tim on the shoulder before sitting down and taking up my hand again.

"Fuck you, Tibby." He didn't have the balls to direct that to Seth.

"No, thanks. There's no telling what you've caught." I held Seth's hand hard, trying to let him know not to get up again. He caught my eye, gave a rueful twist of his mouth. I felt his hand relax.

At that point, the poor girl he was with came over and tugged at his arm, murmuring something to him. She wouldn't meet my eyes, and she wasn't the one he'd been with the weekend I'd met Seth. Wow. He wasted no time. Asshole. The poor girl! She looked like she might die of embarrassment. I would have, if my date was over harassing his ex. Tim let her but glared at me until he sat down again.

"Thank you," I said.

"It was totally my pleasure. What a dick."

"I feel sorry for that girl. I'd be crawling into the floor by now."

Seth shrugged it off. "Don't let it bother you. He's the past." I could tell that he was trying to let it go as well. I liked that, liked that he felt protective. I also liked that he was man enough to let me do things on my own when I knew I could. He didn't make a scene.

"And you're the future?" I teased.

"You know it, baby!"

The waitress came back, eyeing me closely this time. She must have seen Tim making his big stand. Probably wondering what it was about me. Let her. We ordered, and the food came in a decent amount of time.

As we ate, we kept up the easy banter. That was good. Neither of us wanted to get into anything important here. Finally, it was time to go. We left, Seth with his arm around me, radiating possessive good cheer. I liked it.

When we got back to my room, he stretched. "You mind if I get into my PJs? I'm beat."

"Sure." I waited until he had gone into the bathroom, and then changed into my sheer pink nightgown. I wanted this tonight, and I didn't want there to be any ambiguity.

He came back in, carrying his clothes. He didn't look at me as he went to his bag, and stowed them away. Only then did he look up.

I was laying on the bed, arm on my hip. There was no mistaking my intent.

He didn't say anything.

"Are you going to just stand there?" I asked quietly. I hoped I sounded at least a little sexy, but I couldn't tell.

He took off his shirt, which made my heart race. God, that man had amazing abs. My gaze traveled upwards, meeting Seth's eyes. The look in his eyes…I fell into them and was lost. Then he stepped out of his pajama bottoms, and came to the bed, his eyes never leaving mine.

"Are you sure?" His voice sounded a little hoarse.

"So very sure." I held up an arm in invitation, and he slid down next to me. The warmth of his naked body next to my nearly naked body made me feel as though I might burst into flames. He pulled me close to him, and I could feel his hardness close to me. *Not close enough*, I thought. It had gone way beyond physical for me. I wanted to crawl inside his skin, be as close as possible.

Oh, god. I was falling in love with him.

He was of the same mind, because his arms tightened, and he leaned in to kiss me. It was even better than the very first time he kissed me. This time,

I actually saw stars. I lost myself in his kiss. I could cheerfully never leave this bed. Ever.

And then, I saw an even brighter flash.

CHAPTER NINETEEN

I woke up in my room in the present day, again. Oh *shit. Damn it all to hell!* I could feel my teeth grind. It felt like one of those cartoon characters who loses in the end, wringing their hands and muttering, "Foiled again."

The only improvement was that my room didn't smell of pee. I couldn't believe it. Dhameer had a way of making sure I knew what the hell a crossroad was. I didn't get this one though. To me, this just didn't seem like it was that big of a deal. Sex was a milestone in the relationship, sure. But a milestone? That didn't make sense.

As if on cue. Dhameer appeared at the foot of my bed. Perfect timing.

"Okay, how was that a crossroad? Sex? A crossroad? Is this genie humor?"

"I actually don't have control of when the crossroad is reached, Toots."

"What do you mean?" I asked. "This is your gig. You're in charge, here. Of course you have control. I just have to ask how sex was a crossroad, and why it couldn't happen before I got to see him naked." I couldn't tell Dhameer that my heart, once again, felt ripped out by the roots. How had that happened in such a short time?

Dhameer sighed. "All right. Let's go through this so that you understand. What do you think a crossroad is, in relation to your life?"

"A place that a decision sends you down different roads."

"Exactly." He looked at me like I had just solved a math problem.

"That doesn't tell me anything, Dhameer! What do you mean, exactly? Exactly? That doesn't answer a thing! I have had sex with plenty—plenty!—of people. It took things to another level, but a crossroads? Rick asking me to marry him and me accepting is a crossroad. Sex? Not even the same thing!" I leaned back with a huff. I was getting pretty loud, and I wanted to actually talk to him. I figured I had better stop with the yelling.

"Tell me something, Tabitha. What has gone on during your wishes? What is something you have noticed that you didn't expect?"

I thought about it before answering. There had been a lot that I noticed. What was a big thing? I was quiet as I considered what would be the biggest thing.

"I guess that I was learning—well, unlearning—some of the things I learned in the past," I said slowly.

"Such as? Give an example, please." Why did he sound like my worst teacher ever?

"Well, that I didn't have to take the crap dished out by others. Like when Dave and I broke up the first time around, he was so awful. He was as mean as he could be, and he talked so badly about me, saying things that were horrible. I had to deal with that even after he graduated, because people remembered me as a slutty chick who…well, who was easy in certain aspects." I didn't give greater detail because I was embarrassed to repeat it to Dhameer, who didn't seem like he would appreciate hearing about the particulars of what Dave had said.

Dhameer smiled at me. I got the impression he knew what I wasn't saying. "He was an unpleasant boy, that Dave. I was very pleased to see how well you dealt with him this time around. It completely changed school for him the rest of the year. You knew that, though, didn't you?"

"I knew no one wanted to date him. Even the girls who didn't care for me thought that I might be telling the truth, and didn't want to hear about their imperfections while he expected them to take care of him. It was really empowering, realizing that I could just tell him to go to hell, and that if I told others why I did it, it wouldn't necessarily reflect poorly on me if the truth came out."

"What about with your second do-over?"

"That I was right to think that I should have given Seth a chance. That I should have listened to my gut instinct. That risk isn't necessarily a bad thing. That my instinct was right about both Seth and Tim. That I needed to listen to myself. Not only do I not have to put up with crap from those who are supposed to care for me, but that I have good instincts, and I should listen to them. Also, that my friendships are just as important as any relationships with guys," I thought of Danni. Realizing how I'd wrecked things with her was as bad as seeing where I missed out with Seth. This had been when X was working really hard, and we hadn't talked as much. I'd been sad at the time, but it had led me to Danni. Before I ruined it.

"Very good, Toots. Very good, indeed. I am impressed that you have put the two together. I'm also pleased that you expanded your lessons to friendship. Life is very lonely without friends."

"Well, I figured that this would be kind of a stacking lesson. I'm also well aware of how friends bring a lot to your life." I thought about X. If I ended up staying here, in my current life, I was going to move. Be closer to my friend. There was no reason not to be, particularly if I wasn't involved with anyone in this area. I'd only kept away from him because I was so hung up on what a piece of shit I was and hiding myself away from the world. None of that had to be permanent, and I had no intentions of allowing it to be. Not now.

He smiled. "It wasn't planned that way, but that's the way it has played out. No sense in having a wish that allows you to redo parts of life if it doesn't give you the benefit of life experience since then."

"All right, but that doesn't explain what it is you think I am missing here."

"I'll give you two days like I did before to think about what you might be missing, and where you want to go next. You're close, very close, Tabitha." He disappeared in his trademark poof of glitter.

Dammit. I didn't have a clue. I got up, and went about my morning routine, ending with me in the kitchen sipping tea and mulling over my conversation with Dhameer.

What did he mean? Sex was…well, sex was sex. It could be fantastic, sure. Rick was amazing, everything I had ever looked for in a sexual partner. Everything I spent, oh, the next ten years of my life looking for. As wonderful as Seth was, there was something with Rick that was all his. There was also the fact that Dhameer whisked me away before I actually got to try out sex with Seth. I didn't think I was going to get over my bitterness on missing out on that anytime soon.

So what was the deal with sex? Wait. I could be so dense sometimes. I had to literally shake my head and clear it. I went to the counter to grab my pad and a pencil to write things down so I could see this as I worked through it.

I wrote **Lessons** at the top of the paper.

Then, I wrote down *Wish #1*. I wanted to go through this one at a time

1.   I didn't have to be a victim. Was able to shut Dave down before he even really got started.

2.   It was okay to slap down those who would hurt you.

3.   It was okay to take a risk.

All right. That was down. What about with my recent do-over?

Wish #2

1.   I had initially thought I should have called Seth. That was my instinct, and my instinct was right.

2.   I was also right that I had hung onto Tim for longer than I should have.

3.   Don't settle just because it's comfortable

4.   Don't be afraid. See #3 above.

Okay, so I had learned that I could demand better treatment from others, and that I needed to listen to my instinct. That still didn't explain why I hit a crossroad when Seth and I had gotten naked and been heavily into one another and just about to do the deed. Which had been interrupted by my being yanked back to Tibby-Land.

I looked at my list again, tapping my pencil on the pad. It was here, I could feel it. I tapped a bit more, thinking over each point. Then it hit me.

Sex with Rick had been amazing. It was what I'd been looking for ever since, even though in this life, we'd never had sex. It was one of the things I was really missing, the intimacy and connection with another person. He saw me naked in all ways, and still thought I was wonderful. So if agreeing to have sex with Seth was a crossroad, it must mean that it would also be amazing. The lesson in this was that to have sex with someone that loved you was a revelation, a wonder. It had been a revelation with Rick. It pissed me off even more that I had gotten to roll around with Seth a little, gotten to see and touch him, and not actually take things to their conclusion.

So if sex with him was a crossroad, what would have happened? Would I have been with this man forever? Would that have solidified my future with him? Or, would things have faded but I would have been better for knowing him? It was a big what if. I couldn't tell which way things would have gone. That was something I hadn't considered.

Regardless, I had to believe that sleeping with Seth would have brought long term changes, one way or another. Maybe finally being with someone sexually the way I wanted would have shifted the way

I dealt with men from there on out. Hmmm. That was definitely something to ponder.

I looked back at my list. I could add onto #2.

5.   Sex should be something special, to be shared with someone you value who values you as well.

6.   Value your friends—more than anything, no matter how great the guy seems.

How could I have forgotten that? I hadn't gone down the road of losing my close girlfriend. Even though X was my friend throughout, during that time, he'd been working hard to make a name for himself. I'd had to turn to my girlfriends more. I'd actually had to put effort into making some. But when I'd gone off the rails and started trying to heal myself with physical intimacy, it had turned my girlfriends away from me.

It literally felt like a lightbulb had gone off in my head. I almost couldn't put the thoughts together.

7.   The only way to heal and move forward comes from within.

That was what I was missing now. I wasn't allowing myself to heal. Years of fending off the crap my parents handed us via their drinking, and my own insecurities based on shitty guys being awful to me— I'd lost all sense of how to help or heal myself.

The only way I could heal myself was from within. That meant—and I didn't like this bit—that my lack of healing, my living like a hermit—that was all on me. My brothers and sisters reached out, and I ignored them. My parents tried, but were met with anger and they eventually retreated. I had no girlfriends. I kept Xavier, who knew me and loved me anyway, at arms' distance.

That meant that this was all on me. The thought of all I'd suffered at my own hands fell on me like a dark cloud. First no sex, and then seeing that all your misery, all your shit—was all your fault. I felt like downing a case of wine.

But then I realized something. That also meant I could fix and change things. I had already decided that I wasn't going to ignore the lessons I'd learned so far, no matter where I ended up. I could take this a step further and actually make my life better. Not just get along, staying alone and under the radar of everyone. I sighed. No wine this evening.

I wondered what life would have been like had I not been searching for something all those years. If I had felt fulfilled. I remembered telling Rick I wanted to go to law school, and I told Seth that I was interested in law school. I eventually did go to law school, but my own stupidity put me in a place where I didn't feel able to finish. Which really sucked, because by the time I had gotten to law school, I was really excited about it.

I thought about that time. I had come onto campus knowing no one. I got settled in my room but hid out for the next two days. The first day of school brought a big wave of relief for me as I headed for my first class. I sat in that room full of what seemed like hundreds of others, and was nervous. The guy sitting next to me noticed and picked my pen up from where I had dropped it next to him for the third or fourth time.

"Hey, you need a leash for this or something," he said as he handed it back to me.

I gave him a wan smile. He was good looking and had kind eyes. "Thanks," I said. "I guess I am just a little antsy today."

"I get it. It's almost hard to believe you're here, isn't it?"

I wasn't sure if I was supposed to be insulted. I decided not to be offended as I hadn't had any friendly interactions as of yet and didn't want my first interaction with a fellow student to go badly.

"What do you mean?" I asked.

"Well, I don't know about you, but I studied my ass off for the LSAT and waited to see where I could get in, and then I finally got my acceptance here, and then suddenly, here I am in my first class, catching pens being thrown at me." He ended with a smile.

I was glad I hadn't taken offense.

"Yeah, I was so busy worrying about getting in and getting aid, I didn't even think about actually getting here until I was here. I'm Tibby, Tibby Holloway, by the way. Sorry I keep tossing my pen at you."

"Bryant Higgs. It's okay. Is Tibby short for something?"

"Why, is it that bad of a name?" I asked.

He laughed. "No, not at all. I just wondered. You don't really look like an Ey."

"A what?"

"An Ey. You know, WhitnEY, CarEY, BritnEY, LaurIE, BuffY, the EYs."

Now I had to laugh. "No, I am not really an EY, I don't think. It's short for Tabitha."

"I like that, Tabitha. Wasn't that the name of the kid on Bewitched?"

"I think so? I'm not sure. I think you're kind of dating yourself there. Wasn't that a show in the 70s? You don't look that old."

"Gee, thanks, Tibby. You really know how to flatter a person."

"Well, is that your era or not?"

He gave me a look worthy of the snottiest girl in my high school. He even held it for a moment, and we both burst out laughing. It was the start of a tight friendship.

Bryant and I were friends all through law school. Contrary to popular belief, we were not romantically involved. Our third year, we interned over the holiday break together at one of the larger law firms in our area. That was when—

That was it. That was when I wanted to head back to. To the internship, to the annual holiday party for the firm. That was a friggen' crossroad if there ever was one. I hadn't spoken to Bryant since that night. I felt like had I made different choices that night, my life would have been different. I know it would have. This was one place where I could heal. That time in my life, more than anything else, had shaped the past four years. Had sent me hiding under a rock, not wanting to actually come out and live.

Unlike my other wishes, I wasn't sure this one was a romantic one. It could be, but I wasn't sure. Bryant and I had never gone to that place. Would we now? What I was really interested in was what happened to prompt this wish for this time in my life.

I felt like I had done all I needed to do today. I had gone over my lessons learned, and via that, figured out what I wanted to do next. That gave me another day to mull over Seth and how things had gone before I had been so rudely yanked from what would have turned out to be a truly enjoyable time. Dammit. I was still smarting over not being able to consummate things with him. I was also dying of curiosity about how actually having sex could be a crossroad. Did it mean that I would make a decision about staying with sex based on whether the sex was good? I couldn't tell what that said about me. Maybe it was another lesson about being good to myself and getting what I deserved rather than the settling I did throughout my twenties. I wondered whether or not Dhameer would answer any of this or would I have to wait until the end.

While I was frustrated with all the extra questions these wishes were generating, I had to admit it was exciting. When did you ever get the chance to hit your wishful thinkings as the older, and hopefully wiser, you? I knew it was going to be painful and truly sucky at the end of this, just based on what I had felt with Rick and what I could feel was coming thinking about my time with Seth. Still, I was glad that I was getting the chance. I hoped Dhameer heard that, wherever he was, floating around in the ether or whatever it was that he did.

Since I had done the hard work of self-awareness and made the decision on where I wanted to go next, I felt free to go and lounge on the sofa and think about Seth. What might have come after being truly intimate with him? It had been fun traipsing around campus with him. As Seth had predicted several times, Tim had behaved like the tool that he was. Having a handsome and articulate man to squire me around the weekend after we broke up had helped to keep the vitriol from Tim at bay. He'd lied and talked all kinds of shit, but I was able to rise above it and mention *cheating* and *lying* while wishing him well to any mutual friends who asked about our breakup. It put the focus on him rather than me, the way he'd managed to before.

I was surprised that I even had to deal with this. Tim was cheating and when it was discovered, he lost his girlfriend. Makes sense, follows a normal standard of what one might expect. He, however, was all sorts of outraged. He was quite vocal in his outrage, as well. I didn't get it. One more assurance that I was well shot of Tim and all his gyrations.

Seth. I missed him. I hadn't had a year and a half to spend with him like I did with Rick. I didn't have a history with him like I did with Rick. The level and depth that I had with Rick was astounding, especially considering our ages. Even though I knew I was really older than Rick, it was still astounding. It told me that there was something very deep and meaningful in my relationship with him. In spite of the newness of being with Seth, and the somewhat questionable morals I had exercised with moving from a serious relationship to a new one where nakedness was involved within a month or so, I couldn't deny what Rick and I had.

Seth complicated that. I had picked meeting him for my second wish because I had felt a sense of regret that I hadn't called him. Particularly as I knew that I had been holding onto loyalty to a relationship that was one-sided. Hindsight, and all that. It had been everything I had expected. He was just plain hot, and he curled my toes in a way I hadn't expected. His hotness was the whole package. He made me laugh, he didn't shrink from arguing with me. He liked me.

Appreciated me. Expected the best of me, and gave the best of himself. Coming off the heels of being with Rick, I hadn't had any major expectations, but Seth had surpassed them. He was a strong and driven person. He made it clear he wanted to be with me. He was truly a wonderful man.

This was going to drive me to distraction. I had to close the door on Seth also, just like I had done with Rick when I moved onto Seth. I needed to give this third wish my all just like I had done for the first two. Since the first two had resulted in some positive outcomes that I had not expected, as hard as it was, I needed to give do-over three the same chance. I was now missing two different men, two different relationships, and it was going to be hard. I needed to do this, though. I wasn't sure which direction this last wish would head, but I felt like it was a major turning point for me. No, I knew it was. I also wanted to see what it was that I had cheated myself out of.

In looking back, I could see so many places where I had been so dumb! I allowed myself to be burdened with emotions that I really didn't need to burden myself with, which led to relationship choices that affected my entire life. I made choices based on hormones rather than on reason, and it affected my potential to have the career and life that I wanted.

When I had agreed to do this, I didn't expect what a journey of the self this would become. This seemed to go along with the whole premise of what genies were all about. Give you what you wanted, and that meant all the baggage that came with what you wanted. Good and bad, you got it all.

While I felt that perhaps Dhameer had not been as forthcoming with all the caveats that came with his offer, I was glad of it. I realized, with a shock, that even if I ended up with none of my wishes, I would be living my life differently from now on. I didn't need to keep myself hiding away just because I had behaved badly in the past. For the past couple of years, I had kept to myself, attempted to make amends to those I had hurt, minded my own business, and done nothing to anyone else. If someone wished to hold a grudge, well, in some cases, I could completely understand. I had not always behaved in an honorable or even nice fashion. It was the right of those hurt to feel however they wished.

I had attempted to make amends. That those amends were rejected was not on me. I realized that now. For that, I was grateful. Staying here was not going to be the same after this was said and done. I was going to change my life, and lead the life I wanted to without guilt or regret. What that meant specifically, I didn't know. I had some ideas, but I wanted to see what happened next before I made a concrete decision. My perspective had changed so much just from these two do-overs. I was excited to see what the next one might bring.

It could be something really bad, the little nagging voice that was Debbie Doom in my head said. I didn't care at this point. I wanted to share this with Dhameer also. I was sure he kind of knew, being a knowing sort. I was going to tell him anyway.

I looked up and realized it was mid-afternoon, and I hadn't had much to eat. I got up and fixed myself something. Once done, I tidied the kitchen and took a glass and a bottle of wine up to my room.

Not trying to fall back into my boozy ways, I just wanted to drink something comforting and think about the man I had left behind.

I wondered, as I had with Rick, what Seth remembered when he woke up this morning. What was his life like, would remembering me even be all that important? The thought that it wasn't made me tear up a little. I made a mental note to ask Dhameer if, once the final call was made, could he tell me how the choices not taken had ended up. I wanted to know that they were okay, that their lives had still gone onto be something good, and they were living happy lives. That if they had any regrets or doubts, that something could be tossed their way to ease any feelings.

I had a lot to talk about with Dhameer tomorrow. Tonight, something mindless, and perhaps a little soppy, on TV. Tomorrow was going to be an interesting day.

CHAPTER TWENTY

Seth

He shook himself awake. Had he actually fallen asleep at work? That shit needed to stop ASAP. It's what got people killed.

He wasn't at work. He'd been dreaming of back when he was still at the Academy. What was it?

Tibby. He'd been thinking about Tibby. The one who…well, he didn't want to think about it. He hadn't gotten what he wanted, and he'd gone on. He'd thought he might, but he'd been wrong. Way wrong. A year later, he'd asked Will about her, as Will had dated and then married her friend, Danni. Danni said that Tibby broke up with whatever guy she'd been dating and then gotten crazy. He'd gotten the impression that Danni and Tibby had fought, although Danni didn't really say anything bad.

When he'd asked her directly if she had seen Tibby, she shook her head with tight lips. "We're not really good friends anymore, Seth."

That had closed the door on that avenue. Then he'd gotten into flight school and met his wife, and Tibby became one of the things in his past.

So why had he been thinking of her?

Even now, it evoked a wistful, happy feeling. He'd been so sure she was someone special. He still couldn't figure out what had gone wrong there.

The alarm went off. He closed down his musing into the past, and got up to start his day.

***

Dhameer

Another satisfied customer. Which was saying something, as this was getting a bit tricky. He checked in on Tibby. She was all right, as all right as anyone could be. One of the things he regretted was that by giving her exactly what her late night musings and dreams had suggested she wanted, he knew he'd be causing her pain. There was no way around it. Humans never wanted to hear that. They always felt they were so strong, and so capable. They never were. Tibby was doing well, and thus far, she hadn't blamed him for anything except his timing.

He smiled. Her anger at being yanked from the wish at a crucial moment was funny. Well, to him. He wasn't driven by the pleasures of the flesh. He wondered what would have happened if he had been. Some of his brethren had been able to experience physical intimacy. Dhameer couldn't see where it had improved their existence. If anything, it degraded it. Added an unpredictable aspect to a life that was already hard to manage. He was happier without it.

He glanced in Tibby's direction again. She'd made nice progress the night before, and she'd be up soon. Time enough for a check on the first wish, Rick, and then it would be time to see Tibby. He could feel her summons coming.

***

Tibby

When I woke up, I had a slight headache. When I got up, I drank several glasses of water, took a shower, and prepared to face the day. When I had primped as much as I could, and made sure that my house was in relative order, I went back to my room and called out for Dhameer.

He appeared almost instantly, perched on the foot of the bed.

"Morning, Toots. My, you've been a busy girl, haven't you?"

"I figured you heard all that."

"Not all. I do have things to do other than hover over you all day."

"Perish the thought," I said with a grin. "Can we talk before I whoosh out of here?"

"If you like. What would you like to talk about?"

"You said that wishes with you came with a catch, right?"

"Everything has a catch, Toots. It's not an idea unique to me."

"Well, part of the catch is that I don't get to stay. And in the end, I don't make the choice about where I end up, correct?"

"Correct. Where are you headed with this?"

"Does part of how the decision is made include whether or not I pull my head out of my ass and learn something from tripping through time?"

Dhameer didn't speak immediately. "Why would you ask that?"

"I have had a lot of time to think about things as I take road B instead of the road A I took before. I feel like I'm learning things that I should have learned a long time ago."

"Such as?"

"Well, when I was with Rick, I learned that I should have trusted my instincts, and him, and taken the chance. I remember that I was scared, and his blunt honesty made me really nervous. I also remember thinking it would have been hard for me to navigate a relationship with him, but if I had, I would have been better off. I also learned that I didn't have to take shit from people, like I did with Dave when he trashed me. I put up with that crap even after he had graduated and disappeared from my life forever.

When I took a chance to see what happened with Seth, it showed me that once again, I did have good instincts with men. I just didn't pay attention to them, and acted out of fear. I stuck with Tim when I didn't need to. And because first Dave, and then Tim, hurt me, I carried that hurt forward into all future relationships. It was like a big scar that I could never get around.

I also let my friendships go to hell. That was something I hadn't realized until you sent me back there. I didn't take care of my friendships because I was too busy chasing guys and trying to heal something no one else could." I took a deep breath. It felt good and bad to get this out. But once out, once said, I couldn't take this back.

I continued. "I was really pissed when you yanked me just as Seth and I were about to be intimate. I sat here and stewed all night. I couldn't figure out why that particular moment was a crossroads. Then, admittedly after a couple of glasses of wine, it hit me that I had never given sex the proper due. I didn't respect it as a stepping stone for a relationship. It was just part of what happened, regardless of whether the relationship had a chance to be something long term or not. But it really is a big step in a relationship. I'd always heard that, but it never made a real impression in me in regard to my life.

So when I thought about where I wanted to go next, I was thinking that my first two do-overs were definitely romantically related, and I'm not sure that where I want to go next will be focused on the romance. I mean, it could be, but there's no sure thing like there was with Seth and Rick."

Once I finished, I just waited. I felt loads lighter. As though I had let go of a mountain-sized burden. The realization that I had been carrying around so much baggage was both alarming and freeing. Once I realized it was there, I had the choice to let it go, leave it behind. So that is what I was going to do. I was really interested to see what Dhameer would say, whether or not I was onto something or if my rampant navel gazing had finally driven me over the edge of sanity.

Dhameer looked at me for a few seconds before he spoke. "You have indeed been busy. This is more than I thought you would get out of this so far. Good for you. It will make things easier at the end of this."

"That makes me glad to hear, Dhameer. Really glad to hear. Okay, is it time for the next one?"

"You know the drill, Toots."

I closed my eyes and went back to that moment.

I was in the back hallway of the restaurant where the law firm was having the Christmas party. I wasn't alone. One of the senior partners, one of the bad boys, was with me. He had his hands all over me, and we were in the throes of semi-drunken passion.

He was the partner I had been assigned to work with for this internship. I had worked with him all summer and then again during the winter break from school. We had flirted the entire time I had been interning there, and he had followed me back towards the bathrooms as I woozily made my way to the end of the hallway. He had grabbed me and started kissing me, and I figured, what the hell? He was hot, I was single, and it felt good. It was my last year at school, and I knew that he would offer me a job when I graduated.

Oh the stupidity of youth. What I didn't know was that the partner's wife was keeping an eye on him, and having seen him head this way, after observing our less than subtle flirtation, she was on his trail like a bloodhound.

As we were getting more involved, I heard someone come down the hallway. I looked up, although the partner I was with didn't even take notice. It was Bryant. He had a look of near panic on his face.

"Tib! There you are. Come here, and hurry your ass up!"

At that, the partner did look up. "Mind your own business, buddy", he slurred, and then turned his attention back to me. Bryant moved closer, so instead of waving him off like I had before, I kept looking at him. As the guy was trying to kiss me again, I had to shove him a bit.

"What the hell…" he muttered.

"What is it, Bryant?" I asked.

"His wife is headed this way. If she catches you, it won't be him she's mad at. C'mon, Tib. Don't be stupid. Come with me, and save your ass."

"Piss off, you little punk," said the partner, whose name was Gerry.

Bryant ignored him. "Tib, you know I'm here for you. Not like this guy," he said with a look of disgust, glaring at Gerry.

Here it was. This was the moment. Had I told Gerry to piss off, I would not have dealt with the insane fallout of kissing a guy not worth wiping my ass with. His wife had caught us, and instead of rightfully divorcing her loser husband and taking him for all he was worth, she focused on me. While I certainly bore some of the blame, I didn't bear it all. She had made it out as though I had accosted poor, poor Gerry. And Gerry, ass that he was, stood there and let me take the heat by myself. So it was a very bad call on my part, and I had been stupid to choose making out with some guy over a person who had been a friend for a long time and who actually cared about me.

CHAPTER TWENTY-ONE

"You're right, Bryant. So not worth it," I said, giving Gerry and his many hands another shove. "Lead on. Get me the hell outta here."

"I don't think we can. C'mere, and do your best."

"Wha—" but whatever I had said was cut off as Bryant yanked me to him, pulled me towards the other side of the hall into the alcove leading to the bathroom, and laid a kiss on me. None too soon, either. I could hear someone rapidly approaching from the other end of the hallway. The footsteps were angry. I could tell that the owner of the feet was on a mission. Bryant was right. The wife was headed this way, and he had rescued me just in time. I hadn't been sure if this would be romantic. Maybe it would. I tried to concentrate on the kiss, but I found I was shaking with each *click-clack* of the wife's high-heeled step...

"What in the hell?" Said Gerry.

"Gerald!" Said an angry voice. The *click-clacking* stopped.

"What? What, honey? I'm right here," Gerry said, sounding much more alert.

"What are you doing? I've been looking for you everywhere!" Oh, yeah. She was pissed. I didn't remember how angry she was, but I was pretty hazy about most of that night.

"I hadda go to the bathroom!" said Gerry. My lord, he was only one step above a toddler's whine! I had tossed away so much for that? Now I was pissed. How drunk had I been?

"Well, what are you doing standing in the hallway?" She asked.

"They're blocking the door!" he said defensively.

"Excuse me!" said the woman, and I could tell she stepped closer to us.

"Hmmm, sorry?" Said Bryant, breaking away from me, sounding dazed. "Whatdidja say?"

"You are blocking the door to the restroom! Please take this…this whatever it is… somewhere else," she said.

"What? Oh!" said Bryant. "Mrs. Goodman! I'm sorry! We just wanted a little privacy, didn't realize anyone else was here. Sorry about that. C'mon, Tib, let's go home." He looked down at me with an adoring smile.

He was good. Wow. I owed him big. I giggled, so that I looked like a silly girl, and said, "All right, honey. Probably a good idea." I hugged him close, and then smiled up at Mrs. Pinch-Faced Goodman. I could tell she was sure she was going to catch him with me. She seemed disappointed she hadn't. Well she was Gerry's problem, and he was hers.

"Again, sorry about blocking the way." said Bryant.

"Yeah, really sorry," I said with a big smile, making like I'd had a little too much Christmas cheer. "We'll get out of your way now." And I turned to

182

Bryant, squeezing his waist as he pulled me away. We hadn't gone far when we heard the missus start hissing at Gerry. Like I said, his problem. Bryant hugged me close all the way to the end of the hallway. Once we came out into the dining area, he broke away from me but took my hand.

"Let's get our stuff and get the hell outta here," he said. "Keep the cover going."

I nodded, keeping a smile plastered on my face. I could see now why things went the way they did. After Mrs. Goodman had caught me with Gerry, she had blacklisted me with the other wives. They, in turn, had bent their husbands' ears, and I had been let go from the internship. I was a pariah at school, but that didn't last long. Mrs. Goodman, not happy with merely ending my internship, had gone to the Dean and complained, using the Ethics Code against me, and gotten me tossed out of school. Since I had only half a semester to go, it was really hard to try to transfer. What I found when I did try was that my ethics violation had followed me like a bad smell. After a year, I had given up trying, since it seemed like everyone knew I had kissed the old trout's husband.

I wondered how many other young women she had done this to. Gerry didn't seem like a stranger to diddling the staff. What an asshole. As I gathered my purse and my coat, I resolved to find out if any other women had suffered because of the asshole Goodmans. Not excusing fooling around with a married guy, but this had been overboard. What they both deserved was to go broke divorcing one another.

Bryant caught up with me, pulling on his coat. "You got everything? Let's get while we can."

As we left, several of our fellow interns called out. Bryant just waved at them, and I made sure to give them a boozy smile. I could feel the gossip welling behind us. There had been rumors all through school about us, and neither of us would ever admit to anything, mostly because there was nothing there. It didn't stop the gossip, though. Bryant was brilliant. It would look like we had both had a little too much to drink and finally admitted our mad passion for one another, and the whole Goodman fiasco would be a blip on the radar.

We didn't speak until we were safely in his car.

"You. Idiot." He said. "Do you realize how close you came to losing everything? That old bitch would have wiped the floor with you!"

"I am an idiot," I said. "Thank you so much for saving me from myself and my own stupidity."

"You're welcome. What in the hell were you thinking?"

"I wasn't. Well, I was, but not with my head."

"I swear to hell, you're worse than any guy I know."

"Not really. Just a moment of stupid weakness. Which you, being the amazing friend you are, rescued me from."

"Please try to keep your weakness to yourself. I don't want to have to keep rescuing you from cheesy old guys and their harpy wives."

I shuddered. "She was really awful, wasn't she? I don't know why I didn't realize how awful she was. Not that I have much excuse, but damn." Only I knew how awful she would really be, and Bryant had saved me from more than he knew.

"Well I'm sure you and Ger didn't chat about the little woman at home."

I rolled my eyes. "We didn't really chat about anything at all."

"'Course you didn't. He's a total tool."

"Thank you, Bryant." He just looked at me with a disgusted face. "No, seriously, thank you. I think you more than just save me from a tool. I think that old bag would have ruined me."

"I don't know about that. She's gotta be used to Gerry screwing around."

"No, I think she would have gone for blood with me."

"I don't know for sure, but let's say I do so you stop fucking around with married jackasses."

"Deal. You know the gossip is just rolling through the party right now. You're going to have to pretend to have a mad passion for me for a little while."

"I can't tell everyone what a crap drunk you are and just be your friend?"

"Well, sure, but you have to wait a couple of weeks to do it. That way, neither of us get any further beady eye from the dragon lady."

"It'll be tough. I'll do it, but you're gonna owe me."

Ah. "What do I owe you?" My first thought went to something less than savory, but I knew Bryant. He had never once been shitty with me. I didn't think he would now, but...you could never tell with people. Oh, god. Please don't let him be disappointing! Please let me be the loser with crappy expectations.

"You have to take your bar exam with me and then open our own firm together."

I hadn't expected this. I had told Dhameer that I didn't know if this was romantic or not, but that it felt like a turning point.

"You're serious?" I asked.

"Absolutely. I'm focused on international, and you are looking at admiralty. We could form a great practice together. All we need to do is get a couple of really solid clients, and we're in."

I thought about it. I hadn't been sure what I wanted to do, family or maritime. Both were interesting to me, although on completely opposite sides of the legal spectrum. Bryant made a good argument. His international focus with my maritime would allow for us to represent any number of clients who worked globally and had shipping concerns. We could create a niche for ourselves. I doubted we would be rich—not filthy rich, anyway. Well-off, probably. It wasn't necessarily a glamorous field, but both Bryant and I were doing well in our specialties.

It could work. It would keep me away from sleazy partners. I just had to make sure that Mrs. Goodman didn't spread her nasty gossip, as she'd done previously. Hopefully, Bryant's ruse would work. If we let it slip that we were going into business together…I tapped my finger against my mouth. This could work. It would afford Bryant and I the opportunity start something big on our own. Before I went any further with this, I needed to clear my own head on a couple of things. This time around, I would not let sex dictate my life. Even with this chance.

"So, what was that kiss back there? We've never been like that."

"It was to throw off the gorgon. No time for her man if you were busy with your own. Plus, you're my best friend. I can't let you fuck yourself over."

How had I missed this? He was like X, and to an extent, like Danni. I wondered if she and I were still friends in this wish world. I hoped so. But I had no idea. What made me sad was the fact that I thought X was my only friend. He didn't have to be. I'd had more. I just didn't see it.

"That's all it is, though? Nothing more than that?" I tried to keep my tone neutral.

"Do you want it to be more?" Now he turned to look at me, surprise all over his face.

"No, I don't think so. It just took me off guard, and I wanted to make sure that we were clear and there would be no asshurtery or sore feelings tomorrow." I was babbling. Truth be told, I was nervous. I didn't want to have any misunderstandings, and I felt stupid asking him basically if he liked me. Like I should have a note with a Check Here for Yes and Check Here for No box on it.

"None at all. I would have made a move before now if there were."

"Well, I didn't think so, but I was so surprised, I had to ask."

He laughed. "Tib, you're great, and good looking, and fun, but you're not my type."

"What the hell does that mean?" Even though I wasn't interested, I couldn't help feeling a little indignant.

"It means you have good taste in friends such as myself, but you pick shitty men to date. You also have the complication of being a girl," he added, looking straight ahead and not in my direction at all.

Well, he wasn't wrong on the picker. I did date shitty men. But having girl parts—"Wait, are you officially coming out?"

"You don't sound shocked at all," he said dryly.

"I'm not, even though I didn't really think about it. But I don't pry, so I figured you'd tell me something eventually. I didn't want to make you uncomfortable. Whatever you wanted to tell me," I hastened to add. "I thought you had a secret girlfriend, and were keeping her from your student life or something like that."

"Well, at least you didn't toss it in my face when you were drunk."

I couldn't hold my indignation in at that point. "I wouldn't do that! C'mon, Bryant!"

"Tib, you are a bad drunk. Look at what happened just now. You nearly blew it all for some dick."

I wanted to be mad, but he was right. On both counts. I sighed. "You're right. I'm a shitty lush. Why do you want to go into business with me?"

"Because when you're sober and on top of shit, you're awesome. Plus, you're just the person I need to deal with my grandfather."

"What the hell are you talking about?" I wrapped my coat around myself more tightly. Did I just fall into the slutty frying pan from the sort of slutty fire? Was he going to offer me up to his dirty old grandpa?

"My dad is going to go ballistic when he finds out I don't want to go into the family's firm. I want to start my own, and I want you as my partner. You'll help me convince my grandfather to stake us."

"What are you talking about?" Maybe I just couldn't think because the earlier me had consumed far too much alcohol, but this wasn't making sense. Even to the older, wiser me.

"My granddad loves independence. He'll be secretly thrilled that I want to get out from under Dad. But I'll have to convince him to part with money. You're going to help me."

That was better than I expected. "Um. Okay. How?"

"We need to put together a business plan. If we really have our shit together, he'll throw a client or two our way."

"Why doesn't he want you at the family firm?"

"He doesn't care either way, as long as I'm in law. He'd laugh his ass off to see me buck my father."

"Does he know you're…" I raised my eyebrows.

"No. He'll think you're a prospect, which can't hurt. I don't want to tell them." For the first time since he'd gotten me out of the party and off my previous road to doom, he looked uncomfortable. "I'd rather you didn't tell anyone, actually, Tib."

I mimed zipping my lips. "I won't tell anyone. Nor will I confirm or deny that we're a couple."

He looked at me again.

"C'mon! With you dragging me out of there, and then the news that we're going into practice together, the rumors will be flying!"

He laughed. "Maybe that'll save your ass from the Gorgon."

I shuddered. "God, she was fucking horrible!"

"How did you not see her, Tib? You have to promise me one thing."

I glanced at him. "What?"

"I get to vet anyone you want to date."

"What?" My mouth fell open. "You can't be serious!"

He nodded. "Totally. You forget, I've known you all three years of school. I've seen the losers you like. They all suck, Tibby. It's why you let sleazes like Goodman close to you."

I peered at him in the darkness of the car. He seemed angry. Like someone who truly cared about me. Like a real friend. This do-over would be filled with a lot of kicking of my own ass. I could tell. How had I not seen and appreciated Bryant for who he was, and the fact that he truly cared for me? "When you put it that way, I sound like a complete dumbass."

Bryant looked at me, his face serious and intent. "You're such an amazing person, but you never go for anyone who would support you. You always go for guys who shit on you. I don't know why, maybe you'll tell me and get over it someday. Until then, let me meet them before you sleep with them. We'll keep any more Goodmans from happening."

I let my gaze fall to my clasped hands. My face was red, I could feel it. I was ashamed. Had he thought this back then? It was true. I didn't like to admit it, but it was. Which meant I'd been trying to fix the damage from Dave, and Tim, and…oh shit. I probably wasn't friends with Danni. The thought made me sad.

In my other life, I hadn't seen Bryant since law school. I didn't know what he had done. I remembered that I would see him around after the party, and he would have a wistful expression. Maybe it was because of this? The lost opportunity? That made me even sadder.

Suddenly, I was so glad that I had chosen this moment. I initially chose it because I couldn't think of another time when I'd faced a choice. The other two had been romantically based. This one, this was just for me. For who I might become.

How...serendipitous?—that Bryant had already figured out what it took me years and a couple of wishes to see. I'd be a fool not to take him up on this. As sexually deprived as I'd been feeling, as painful as my first two wishes had been in some aspects, I was doing something here that was for me alone

The thought was exhilarating.

"Bryant, let's go see your grandfather whenever you want. I'm thrilled that you want to work with me, even knowing all my dirty laundry."

"You wanna go tonight?"

"Sure. Would he be up for it this time of night?"

Bryant shrugged. "He'd probably take us less seriously."

"Then let's not. Let's set up a lunch meeting with him. After we've had time to set up a study schedule and after we can show him we've registered to take the bar. We also need to come up with a business plan." I stopped, thinking about what the head of a major DC firm would want to hear from us. What would make him back us financially? I didn't realize I'd been silent the rest of the ride home until I noticed that Bryant had pulled up to my apartment building.

"Come in. I won't be able to sleep. Let's get some of this on paper tonight!" I couldn't help my enthusiasm.

Bryant laughed as he followed me into the lobby. "This is why I wanted you, Tib. Look at you. The wheels are already going a million miles an hour!"

I reached for him to give him a one armed hug as we walked up the stairs. I had your typical student apartment, which meant elevators thousands of years old that never worked anyway. Tonight, however, nothing bothered me. This was the sort of second chance I hadn't expected for myself, and I didn't want to waste a moment. The fear of not knowing when Dhameer would pull me out propelled me forward as well. I wanted this to be as viable an option as the first two.

"You're going to have to drive me back to my car," I said over my shoulder as we walked into my apartment. A glance around was enough to tell me that I had been having one of my neat spells before I fucked up and made out with my boss. The place was presentable. I sighed inwardly, glad that untidy messes were not an immediate concern.

Bryant knew the old me well. "You picked up, huh? What prompted that?"

I scowled. "I can be neat."

He snorted.

"When I want to."

"I'm glad it's sort of a habit. You're going to have to make it a regular habit," he said, sitting down at the table. "So talk. I can practically see the smoke. What's on your mind?"

"Well, first we need to register to take the bar."

Bryant held up a hand. "I've already done it. YOU need to do so tomorrow."

I rummaged in the kitchen, coming up with a pad of paper and a pen. I joined Bryant at the table.

Register for bar, I wrote at the top. I met his eyes. "What next?"

"We need to figure out what we're going to need to set up shop," He leaned back in the chair, thinking. "When's your lease up?"

"I'm on a month to month. I have been since last year."

"Perfect. We're going to maximize our assets."

"It's late, Bryant. Speak English, please." I put down the pen and glared.

"Okay, okay! My grandfather has a number of townhouses in Georgetown. I bet we can ask him to rent one. We'll use the top floor as a place to stay, and then we'll have the offices downstairs. Not that we can do anything right now, but it'll set us up."

I didn't write that down. "Bryant, I have the tiny little stipend from the internship and my savings from over the summer. It's enough to get me by until the next summer. It's not enough for me to live on with Georgetown rent!"

"Don't worry about it. We'll get the family discount," he said with a grin. "And Tibby?"

"What?"

"I get to decorate. Damn, girl," he looked around. "This is truly wretched." He rolled his eyes. "No jokes about stereotypes!"

"I wasn't even going there. I was thinking, 'Whatever'. I'm on a tight budget. And decorating is just not my thing." I thought about how I'd grown up. Mom and Dad couldn't care less about pictures on the wall. I used to bring home my art projects and hang them up just to have something. The last time I'd gone home, a few of them still hung in the kitchen, faded and showing signs of being stained with something. Probably another fight where Mom's food was tossed around for not meeting Dad's standards. Whatever the hell those were. No one knew, least of all him. My parents put on a good show outside the house. Once inside, the mask dropped.

I shook my head to clear it of the musings of my perpetually fucked parents. I couldn't do anything about that now. I reminded myself that not everything was black and white, and perhaps my parents were not the lost cause I'd thought. Nor did I want to think about how making out with the partner had cost me this, something that had the chance to be wonderful.

I was so stupid when I was younger. And I wasn't that much older now. Just wiser and far more melancholy.

Bryant and I talked all night, finally stopping when dawn was breaking out my patio window.

"We need some sleep." I couldn't hold in the massive yawn.

"I'm going to go home and call my granddad today. Let's meet with him tomorrow, Tib," Bryant's enthusiasm was undimmed.

"Okay. I'm done by one. Can he do a late lunch?"

Bryant laughed. "He's the senior founding partner. He does whatever he wants."

"What a nice place to be. You need to go. I'm about to fall over."

He stood, and pulled me up with him. "Go to bed. And Tib?"

"Yeah?"

He kissed me fast on the forehead and headed for the door. "This is the right decision."

I smiled at him in spite of how tired I was. "I totally agree."

He shut the door quietly behind him. I fell into bed and slept until nine that night.

CHAPTER TWENTY-TWO

The next morning, Bryant caught up with me in between classes. I noticed that several of our classmates had knowing grins on their faces. I ignored it. I'd already gotten the third degree from Monique, one of the interns who was in my Trade Law class earlier. I'd blushed and said as little as possible. Nothing about Bryant and I going into business. I knew she'd gossip her head off, which was fine with me. Anything to keep Gorgon Goodman off my ass.

"I set us up for 1:30 at his club. Meet me after class, and I'll drive us over."

"His club? What is this, merry old England?"

Bryant laughed. "You have no idea. You have all our plans?"

I patted my leather case. "Right here. I haven't let them out of my sight."

"Good. I'll see you later."

I watched him run off, and I felt better than I had in some time. Losing the chance to go further with either Rick or Seth had been depressing. I tried really hard, but I loved Rick and cared a lot for—was falling in love with—Seth. It hurt to leave when I did. This was different though. This was something just for me. It was something that didn't depend on what a man thought of me—well, it kind of did, but not romantically. I'd allowed the romantic considerations to be so much of who I was and what I did, that to be considering something else felt almost like foreign territory.

But I liked it. I was excited to meet with Bryant's grandfather.

I'd have to make sure I did a little primping before lunch. I'd worn a suit today, just in case he'd been able to schedule it. It was the right choice. Bryant had a suit on as well.

***

"Why is it you think I want to support this foolish idea?" Mr. Higgs leaned back in his chair. We'd had a pleasant lunch, the dark tones of Mr. Higgs' club giving the meeting weight. Not that it needed any more weight than it already had.

Bryant had brought up the subject of our firm during lunch, but Mr. Higgs ignored it. Now, over crème brûlée and coffee, he went in for the kill. It was an effective tactic. He was hoping to catch us off guard, find a chink in our plans. I could see why Bryant wanted a little backup.

"Because it's a solid plan," I answered, leaning forward on my elbows and lacing my fingers. I kept eye contact with him. "We've got a good plan for managing expenses, both personal and business. We developed an actionable plan for building the business once we're both out of school. There aren't a lot of firms that specialize in what we want to. It will be a place to send clients. Somewhere that you have a family connection."

"Hoping to be part of the family?" He asked gruffly. Wow. I wasn't expecting that. Bryant looked as though he wanted to sink into the floor.

"Granddad, really." Bryant's face turned bright red, and he wouldn't look at me.

I kept eye contact with the old guy. This was bait.

Mr. Higgs waved his protest away. "It's a legitimate question. What if things go south with you two? Seen it happen before with partners. Add in the romance, and it has an even greater chance of going belly up. Then where am I? Where's my money?"

I jumped in. "We're not involved, Mr. Higgs. I do love Bryant. He's one of my best friends. But there's no romance there."

He narrowed his eyes at me, glaring. I didn't blink, didn't move an inch. "Hmmphh." He turned back to Bryant. "What guarantee do I get regarding repayment?"

We'd prepped for this. "We're prepared to offer you terms of ten years if our business is up and going strong, twenty if we fold." He was ours. He just hadn't admitted it yet.

"Not much return on investment." The old man crossed his arms. Neither of us spoke. This was it, the moment where we needed to shut up, and let him make up his mind. We'd given him all our arguments, countered his concerns. I moved my foot and carefully applied pressure to Bryant's foot, mentally imploring him not to speak another word. Now it was up to him. I hoped like hell I hadn't misread him just now.

"Well." He banged his hands on the table and stood up. "Bryant, I think you've got a solid start. You and Tabitha come and see me next week. I'll have the papers drawn up and sent over before then. I'll get one of the townhouses cleaned, too. You both can come into the office and take care of the papers. There's one condition, though." I saw his eyes twinkle and his mouth turn up slightly.

Bryant must have seen this before, because I saw his shoulders rise up a little. A sure sign of stress. "What?"

"Once we sign it all, we call your dad in. I'll even add him to my calendar." The old guy actually rubbed his hands in glee.

"Why is this so enjoyable to you?" I had to interject. I felt for Bryant. This old man was a button pusher of the highest order.

"Hasn't Bryant told you? Love all my kids, but my son has a major stick up his ass. Thinks his way is the only way. I'm a downright embarrassment, but he can't bitch too much because it's still my firm. Bryant is not compliant and appreciative, so he's troublesome. No law against a man helping his grandson, and that will piss Franklin off more than anything. Hates to have someone else driving the bus. Be prepared," he added, his face suddenly serious. "He'll demand the papers and try to find a way out. Carry on like a wailing woman, and make us all miserable for a time. You, too, missy." He shook his finger at me. "But you both are prepared, and have a good, solid plan in place. Not *too* much risk and a good backer." His eyes twinkled again. "We'll see how you do on the bar exam. I might have a client or two for you. Call me when you get the paperwork, boy." He patted Bryant on the back, gave me a small bow, and walked from the dining room.

"Wow. You're weren't kidding." I swear, he practically danced out the front door. No wonder Bryant needed backup.

Bryant sagged in his chair. "I wasn't sure he was going to say yes."

"I knew he would. When he started asking really pointed questions, it was all over but the fuss. He's delighted to help you, Bryant." I hadn't seen Bryant this rattled very often. I wanted to help him calm a little. What would meeting his dad be like?

"Thanks for being here with me."

"Thanks for asking me. Seriously, I'm so grateful. We're going to kick some major ass."

Boy, did we.

As predicted, Bryant's dad nearly blew a gasket. I thought his grandfather was going to burst something, he was so tickled. But it was an ironclad document. I knew it. We'd haggled over it—the old guy had slipped some less than fantastic terms into it. I kind of thought he was testing us.

We both studied our asses off, and passed the bar on the first try. Once we did, Mr. Higgs kept his word and sent clients to us. We did well with them. It seemed as though overnight we had a healthy number of them. Bryant handled the details. He could recall the minutest of facts accurately. I was the better negotiator, and together we did well by our clients.

So much so that less than three years in, I was able to buy a sailboat. I still stayed at the townhouse, but I spent as much time on my boat as I did there. Bryant and I needed space. I still had my Thing. He teased me unmercifully about it, but I wouldn't get rid of it.

And for three years, I hadn't dated anyone. I'd gone on dates, and as I'd promised Bryant, I let him vet them. He disliked all of them. So I didn't let it go any further, even though the lack of emotional and physical intimacy sucked.

Sounds crazy, I know. But I'd promised, and since I was still in this life and had determined to make the most of it for me, I wasn't letting my penchant for bad boys and assholes ruin it.

I'd called out to Dhameer occasionally, but he never responded. I guess I hadn't hit a crossroads yet. It made me wonder again what he considered a crossroads. I felt like I ran into them several times over the past three years, but apparently not by his standards. I also took the step of making some kind of peace with my parents. What I found was that while they would probably never completely apologize for all the shit we put up with from them, they were trying in the only way they knew. It wasn't always pretty, and sometimes it totally sucked. But at last, I'd found some peace with them. No longer did I feel hostage to their choices, their baggage. I had a choice as to whether or not I carried it, and I chose to put it behind me. It was a freeing feeling. If I ever hit a crossroads and ended up where I was three years ago, I'd make the effort. I promised myself that.

I had, in this timeline of events, lost touch with Danni. Because in this, I broke up with Tim after discovering his cheating months after I met Seth. I went down a path Danni didn't like—and we'd drifted apart. Last time I'd spoken with her, in my senior year in college, she'd still been with Will. Neither of them ever mentioned Seth to me. I didn't ask. I had Xavier still. Like before, once I passed the bar, he called me and hired me on the spot. Now, in addition to double checking his books and his finances, I handled his legal affairs. Gone right out and taken an entertainment law class, just for him. I was thrilled. I asked Dhameer to ensure that he was in my life, no matter where I was, and here he was.

One thing I hadn't done was to look up Rick or Seth. I couldn't. Sometimes I thought about it. Put their names in the search bar and almost hit *Enter*. But I couldn't. I didn't want to see their happy lives, their wives and kids. I just didn't. I know it was stupid, but I couldn't. Better to wonder and have a teeny bit of hope, than know and have none.

Bryant came into my office, cutting short my musings. "I just got a call from Granddad."

By now, I called the old guy Granddad too. He treated me like one of his grandkids. Even Bryant's dad was coming around.

"What's up?"

"He has a case he needs help with. An old friend having a dispute with Barrington Shipping."

"Have we worked with them or against them before?" The name rang a bell, but only a faint one.

"Nope. They're up in Massachusetts, old company. It's an old guy who runs it. I heard he's got one of the kids or grandkids coming in to help him, but that's all I know. For now."

"Okay. Let's find out all we can about them. What's the beef?"

"Freight charges, disagreement over contract language."

"He wants us to take on that? Seems a little like overkill." I was puzzled. This wasn't really anything that a good contract attorney couldn't sort out. We were specialized, which meant more money. Why would he do that to a friend?

"Yeah, but his friend is pissed Granddad isn't

handling it. Granddad chickened out and lobbed it to us."

"Does he know our rates?"

"He pays Granddad's," Bryant said.

Oh, well. Then we were a bargain. "Okay. Let's get to it."

We set up a meeting for the next week. Granddad's friend was fuming mad, and not willing to wait. I sighed. Granddad had no friends that were normal, sane, or calm.

Present day

Which brings us to right now. When I walked into the room, and introduced myself to Clifford Barrington, and twin voices exclaimed, "Tibby?"

CHAPTER TWENTY-THREE

I felt faint, and like I couldn't catch my breath. Were Rick and Seth really standing there, looking at me? They both were slightly open-mouthed. I knew I probably looked the same. I pulled my professionalism around me like a cloak.

"Gentlemen. I am called Tibby, although in less formal surroundings."

That seemed to snap both of them out of it. Rick recovered first. He held out a hand to Bryant.

"Rick Montevaldo, attorney of record for Mr. Barrington."

Bryant shook his hand and glanced at me. "My pleasure, Mr. Montevaldo. I take it you know Ms. Holloway?"

I stepped into the breach here. Grasped Rick's hand. "Indeed we do. He was good friends with my neighbors growing up." I squeezed his hand warmly. I felt Bryant's brow raise inquiringly behind me. I didn't even need to see it. He knew my parents, knew how I grew up.

Mr. Barrington drew Seth forward. "This is my grandson, Seth McKay. He's agreed to come on board with me, finally."

"Mr. McKay," Bryant was saving my life here. They shook hands and then Seth turned to me.

"Tib—Ms. Holloway, it's good to see you again."

Seeing him now, right in front of me, next to Rick brought back all the loss from my first two wishes. Why in the hell wasn't Dhameer whisking me away? How did this not count as a crossroads? My god. They both looked fantastic, good enough to eat. I had to stop the direction of my thoughts. They were not businesslike at all.

I shook his hand, covering it with my other hand. "Mr. McKay. It's a pleasure to see you again. We met back when we were both in college," I said for the benefit of everyone else there. And to cover the avalanche of feelings that were at play within. Holy hell. Rick and Seth. They knew one another. We were all in the same room.

This must be what it felt like to implode. I plastered a grin on my face. I'd get through this if it killed me.

Barrington was obviously a bit perplexed by all this. "Well? Very nice to know you all know one another. Makes things easier. Should we get to it? This really shouldn't be a difficult matter to fix."

"Of course not," I switched my attention to him. We'd banned our client from attending with us, given his temper.

"Your client isn't with you?" Rick asked, almost as though he was reading my mind.

"We are fully authorized to represent his needs and wishes," Bryant said smoothly. I had to smile. He was good at the socially awkward times we occasionally found ourselves in at work.

"Damn good thing, too" said Barrington. "Likely to burst a blood vessel just trying to get past hello," he finished in an audible mutter.

I had to stifle my laugh. It was an accurate representation of Barney Templeton.

"Be that as it may, we do need to sort this out before anything can move forward," said Bryant. "What, exactly, do you dispute regarding Mr. Templeton's claims?"

And with that, we were off into business. Occasionally, I could feel the weight of Rick, Seth, or both of them glancing at me, as well as questioning looks from Bryant. Oh, the after work discussion was going to be just fabulous. It made me want to sigh already.

"Well, I think that we'll be able to bring this to our client and have an answer for you by week's end, gentlemen," I said, gathering the papers up and putting them in my case. "We thank you for meeting with us. You'll hear from us soon." All I wanted was to get out of there. I wasn't ready for talking to either one of them. I'd bet my cell had messages on it by end of day, though.

I was out the door after a brief round of handshakes. Bryant had to hurry to catch up with me.

"Tib! C'mon! What the hell?" He touched my arm as he came abreast of me.

I stopped. "You really want to know? It's a long damn story."

"I really do."

Just then, my phone rang. I didn't recognize the number. "Hello?"

"It's Seth. I want to see you, Tibby." His tone suggested he wouldn't take no. I felt a trill of…fear?

Excitement? I wasn't sure what. Nor why. I hadn't done anything wrong. But—

"How did you come by this number?" I asked, stalling.

"My company has your contact info. I finally looked at it. The minute you left the office."

He didn't want to fool around with the social niceties. I could feel it. Okay, I can agree to that. When and where?" I didn't say his name. I didn't want more questions from Bryant than I could handle.

"Tonight. Near your office. I've cancelled the rest of my afternoon. As soon as I drop off my grandfather I'm heading towards your office."

It sounded like a promise. My face warmed at the thought. At that moment, I missed him terribly—all that I'd shared with him, all that I wanted to share.

"I'll get in touch when we get back to the office," I managed.

"Don't stand me up, Tibby."

"I won't. Thanks for calling." I hung up before he could get another word in.

"Who was that?"

"No one I want to talk about right now." I avoided Bryant's gaze.

"Which one of them was it?"

Now I did look at him. I noticed that we'd made it back to his car. He opened the door, and we got in. "What are you talking about?" I asked as I buckled my seatbelt. Thank god Bryant was the one driving today. I wasn't aware of much beyond a foot past my nose.

"Don't try and run your game on me, Ms. Holloway. Which one of those guys just called you?"

Before I could answer, the phone rang again.

Christ. "Hello?" I didn't recognize the number, but I would bet—

"Tibby, this is Rick. I couldn't believe I walked in there and saw you. I'd love to see you. Soon. When can we get together?"

He must have gotten my number from the files, too. Didn't they look at shit before meeting with the other side? I shook my head. I knew they didn't. We didn't. We didn't care who repped the other side. We couldn't be the only firm that took such an approach.

"Um. I don't have my calendar, but maybe tomorrow, after work?"

"Fine. I'll come downtown and meet you."

"Will you send me an email to remind me? We can work out the details." I was sure my email address was listed in the work file, too. Along with my cell number.

"I will. I can't wait to catch up with you." His voice was warm. Remembering all the times I'd heard that tone, my face warmed as well. Damn it. I knew Bryant was watching all this.

"I feel the same," I said. I couldn't stay all business. Not with the memories just his voice could evoke.

He hung up without a good-bye. He'd always been like that. I hit *End* and turned to face Bryant.

"That was the other one, wasn't it?" His tone was mildly accusing mixed with humor.

"You're laughing at me?"

"Tib, watching those two pant over you was the funniest thing I've seen in ages. Well, almost the funniest thing. The funniest thing was watching you try to ignore them. You could have cut the tension with a knife in there. Barrington was grinning behind his hand the whole time."

"Holy hell. That's just fantastic." If this made the rounds—

"How do you know them?"

"Um…" I tried to focus. My heart was racing still, just from touching their hands. Hearing their voices after all these years. I thought I'd managed well over the past three years, but that simple touch from both of these men told me that perhaps I was wrong. Now that I didn't have to be on point in a meeting, my head was doing cartwheels at the thought that all three of my wishes had collided. That I'd had no glitter shower to drag me away and leave me frustrated and crumpled with the weight of my feelings. "I really did kind of grow up with Rick. We flirted like crazy, but…" my voice trailed off. Visions of the year I spent with him flashed in front of me. I couldn't tell Bryant that, though. "Nothing ever happened," I finished in a small voice.

"And McKay?"

"I met him one night out with my friends. He laid this kiss on me, and then gave me his number. Because I was dating this total loser, and I was stupid and blind, I didn't take him up on it, didn't call him." I could see Seth, standing naked in front of me, looking at me with his feelings in his eyes just like it was yesterday and my entire body temperature felt like it rose a full degree. I knew my face was as red as a beet.

"Well it's obvious none of you have forgotten each other. How do you think they know one another?"

"I don't know," I said impatiently. "Probably from some 'Karma for Tibby' set up."

Bryant laughed so hard he almost had to pull over. He'd calm down, and then be off again, laughing until tears rolled down his face. We made it back to the office alive, where he opened the car door and just leaned out of it, laughing.

"This is not fucking funny, Bry! What the hell am I going to do?" I could hear panic in my tone, and that stopped me. No one but me knew that I'd had two wishes where I got to know both these guys up close and personal. No one. As far as Rick knew, he hadn't seen me in ten plus years, and I'd been the dewy little seventeen year old neighbor of his best friend. Seth? I was a girl he'd met one night seven years ago. I wasn't anything more than a blip on their radar, a pleasant memory of the past. I could meet both Rick and Seth, answer the *what the hell* questions about the past, and manage, one way or another.

I'd decide after I met with them. There was nothing to panic over, nothing to be upset over. Only I held all the info, only I knew the score. I laughed to myself at my bravado. Easier said than done.

"Why don't you come in when you've pulled yourself together?" I said frostily to Bryant. I stalked into the office. Some best friend. I needed support right now, not his hysterical laughter. This would also give me time to call Seth.

Once I'd safely hidden myself in my office with the door closed I flipped through the numbers on my phone, and called him back.

"Tibby?"

"We just got back. How familiar are you with the area?"

"Enough. Where do you want to meet?"

"Let's meet at O'Hare's." That was close but far enough away that I wasn't guaranteed to run into anyone I knew.

"I'm heading there now. Don't take your time. I want to see you."

"Okay."

He hung up. When had he started doing that, ending the call without saying good-bye? Just like Rick. How much time had he and Rick spent together? I flinched at the thought of what they might have talked about. Then I stopped myself. This was a runaway train. I had to get off it, right now. This wasn't something you were likely to share with others. I hadn't even told Bryant or X, and they were my besties. An attorney and client weren't going to be sharing this sort of thing—a fleeting memory from the past. To them, I was no big deal. Or at least, I shouldn't be. So why, then, had both called me immediately? Wanting to get together. I shook my head.. *Pull it together, Holloway.*

I forced myself into the restroom so I could tidy up. I always kept a change of clothes and full make up at the office. You never knew when you'd need to do repair, or how much. Now the goal was to get out before Bryant cornered me. I made it back to my office and was locking up when—

Too late. He poked his head in my door. "Spill, sister. Which one are you going to meet just as soon as you can give me an excuse?"

I hung my head. "Seth."

He laughed, and I threw a pen at him. "It's not funny!"

211

"Oh, yes it is! It's hilarious. For the record, I think they're both decent, so you're allowed to go out with either one. Or both. You have my permission." He gave me a regal wave and walked out. Almost immediately, he popped back in. "You can leave now. No lame-assed excuse needed."

He ducked as another pen went flying.

***

I was muttering to myself as I searched for parking around O'Hare's. I could feel the sweat beading all over me. All I needed was for Seth to see me soaked with nervous sweat. Yay. That would so fantastic, huh?

It had been years since I'd seen him as someone I was dating, and he was still in my mind's eye, clear as could be, beautiful and perfect and totally into me. I hadn't really dated anyone since which, if I thought about the way I used to be, was some kind of miracle. I found that I loved my life, even without a significant other. I missed the closeness, and visions of Seth nearly sent me over the edge, but I had my two good friends and a good life. Did I want to let Seth into that? I had a pretty good thing going.

I hated that I didn't have an answer to that question. I loved my life. I thought, when I left him, I could love Seth. Wait. I had to remind myself, *he doesn't know anything. Or remember anything.* So it's a fresh slate, in spite of all this 'meet me immediately' stuff.

As I walked into the bar, I resisted the urge to wipe my palms on my skirt. I hadn't been this nervous since my first trial in front of a judge. I spotted Seth in a booth at the back, and I walked quickly to him, then stopped. He looked up at me. I stood there, frozen. We looked at one another without speaking. If we kept this up, it was going to get awkward.

"Join me?" He asked finally, breaking eye contact and gesturing towards the table.

"Yes, I'd...I'd like that." I forced myself to move, to sit down across from him. My voice was husky. The atmosphere was charged in a way it hadn't been when I saw him at the meeting earlier.

He gestured towards the bar and one of the bartenders came over.

"Laphroaig, please. On the rocks." I didn't drink scotch often, but this situation called for it.

"We have the ten year, if you like," said the bartender.

"Please."

He nodded and left.

"I wouldn't have pegged you for a scotch drinker," Seth said slowly.

I couldn't tell him that I'd had it with him when we went to Harry Browne's on our first date that lasted all day. That I'd started drinking it as a tribute to him. So I lied. After a fashion. The memories of that night surrounded me, and I took a deep breath before I answered. *No one else knows, no one else knows.* "I tasted it in college, and I liked it. It seemed appropriate."

"Why would you say that?"

"Why did you call me, demanding to meet tonight?" My voice actually sounded calm, and more like the professional me. *Good one, Tib!*

"What would you say if I told you I was dreaming of you recently? And then you walk into that room, and there you are, in the flesh. Almost right from my dream. What can I say? I was struck, just like…" his voice trailed off, and then he continued. "Just like the last time I met you."

"I'd say maybe your subconscious knew you were going to meet me. I don't know, Seth. Whatever it is, you need to keep it together when we're meeting for business. My partner was full of questions, and apparently your grandfather and your attorney were as well." Oh, hell. I sounded like an angry teacher.

"That's another thing. I wasn't aware that you knew my attorney." His eyes narrowed.

"I wasn't either. I haven't seen Rick Montevaldo since high school. My partner handled facilitating this meeting. It was rather last minute, due to…" I stopped, not wanting to sink our client by saying that he basically threw a fit and Gramps tossed us to the wolves. "I also don't know what that has to do with anything."

Seth nodded, accepting my explanation. He seemed to be struggling with what he wanted to say. He took a drink of his beer and then spoke. "So. What did you do after…that night we met?"

"I went back, finished out the year, and decided that I wanted to go to law school."

"Didn't you still have a couple of years of school left?" He was distracted. Fiddling with the drink napkin, not looking at me directly. Apparently, there was a lot going on upstairs.

It made me feel a little better that I wasn't the only one. But how odd that he was so bothered by meeting me one night. He didn't have all the memories that I had playing in my mind. "I did. But choosing a grad school path tends to get the parents off your ass. Made my last year of school a lot less stressful," I smiled. "What about you? I thought you were headed to flight school?" Oh shit. Had we talked about that in the pizza place? I couldn't remember. *Please let me get through this*, I begged, not sure who I was asking.

Seth didn't look surprised, so maybe he had mentioned it. "I did. I put in my time, and then my grandfather asked me to come and work with him. My mom's not interested, and he wanted someone in the family to take over for him. She's his only child, so that pretty much leaves me as the take-over candidate." There was a glimpse of that megawatt smile.

"He's got a solid reputation in the business. You're stepping into some big shoes," I said. It sounded so lame, but I didn't know what to say. I was overwhelmed. The fact that I could make small talk was some kind of miracle. I kept seeing him that last night, and the pain and ache roared back. And the lust. It swirled around in me like a tornado. He was just as fit and handsome and charming, even with his obvious distress, as he'd been when I'd met him.

It wasn't only lust for the physical. Like it had been in the second do-over, it was a lust for the man, the person he was. I didn't know this person, though. There was no guarantee this man and the Seth I knew were the same. What had his past been like after I turned him down? I knew more than most how even small things could change a person. He looked, sounded, god, even *smelled* like the Seth I'd known, but that wasn't a guarantee.

"I'm sorry. This must be awkward for you," he said. "With you being the attorney for Gramps' rival. Well, rival right now. They'll be friends again in two weeks."

"Ah. I see you know my client well," I said with a smile.

We made idle chitchat for another twenty minutes or so. My drink was almost finished. There was a feeling of unfinished business. I couldn't tell if it was mutual, but I definitely felt it from my side. The fact that it might only be coming from my side made me really uncomfortable.

It felt like neither of us were really saying what we wanted to. Every time he spoke, or became animated, I kept seeing the guy I'd spent time with, and the last time we'd been together. When he was naked. Looking at me with love and anticipation. God. I had to stop. Clear him out of my head. It wasn't working.

"Well, looks like I'm nearly done. I probably shouldn't have another, so…" I looked down at the table. I didn't know what to say. "I think I'm going to go now. It was good to see you, Seth." Damn. Damn, damn, damn! Not a thing had been resolved. Not one thing. He'd been so intent on seeing me—why? Nothing really important had been said. What the hell? While I felt I needed to get out of there, my heart broke a little as I stood. This wasn't how I saw things going.

"Okay." He stood up quickly. Too quickly. Obviously he was having second thoughts. I didn't know if that made me happy or sad. He tossed some bills on the table. "I'll walk you to your car."

I nodded, my smile tight. We headed out of the bar in silence. Once I reached my car, I turned to him, hand out. "I'm glad we cleared the air." Even though we hadn't cleared a goddamned thing.

He looked at my hand, and then into my eyes. "Fuck it," he said, and taking my hand, he pulled me to him hard and kissed me.

His kisses hadn't changed. Not one bit. If anything, they were better. Of course, that could also be due to my sexual drought, but I didn't think so. This was entirely due to Seth.

My knees nearly gave out, and I reached a hand out behind me to brace myself against the car.

As suddenly as he'd kissed me, he let me go. I fell back, still not able to stand unassisted. He stared at me, his breathing heavy. So was mine. I was sorry he'd ended the kiss.

"I can taste the Laphroaig on your tongue," he whispered. His voice was so soft, I almost missed his next words. "Like before."

Then his eyes widened, and without another word, he turned and stalked away. Like before? What in the holy hell did he mean?

I didn't have a chance to find out, because at that moment, as the weight of his words sank in, as a thought began in my head, the flash I'd been expecting for the last three years blinded me to everything around me.

CHAPTER TWENTY-FOUR

"You have got to be kidding me," I said loudly as my old room came into focus. "Have three years addled your brains? How in the hell was that anything other than awkward as ass?"

Dhameer appeared, although this time he was perched on my dresser. How cute. Like a parrot. Waiting for a damn cracker.

"You are an attorney now, correct?"

I nodded.

"And your career is based on reading others?"

"In part."

"Then please tell me what you noticed right before you came back here. Think, Tabitha."

I wanted to argue with him, fuss and carry on. I was as just as upset about Seth as I was about the entire rest of my life. I'd worked hard for that life. I'd learned my lessons. I'd earned everything I had, fair and square. I'd made a life I was proud of. I'd had my three wishes converge in way that might have turned out well. I wanted to scream at him over the unfairness of it all.

I took a deep breath and forced myself to go over the entire meeting with Seth. Reliving that kiss was hard. God, I wanted him so badly. All of him. I'd managed until his kiss reminded me of exactly how long it had been since I'd seen him. The possibilities that had overwhelmed me the last time I'd seen him had come roaring back like a freight train. That was out of the question too, since here I was, back at Tibby Loserville Central.

Wait. Wait. His last words, the words he said as he stopped kissing me, before he ran away. I closed my eyes, wanting to see as much of it as possible.

"*I can taste the Laphroaig on your tongue. Like before.*"

I opened my eyes, and stared at Dhameer. "What did he mean, just like before?" I whispered. The thought was so big, I couldn't get my head around it. This was what I'd been thinking when he dragged me back. I needed to hear it from someone else.

"When would he have experienced that?"

Oh my lord. "He was there? I mean him him, like the way I was there?"

"So it would seem."

"So it would seem? What does that mean? This isn't a hard question, Dhameer! Was Seth in a do-over thing like me? Was he using a wish? Is that why he said that? Because he *remembers*?" My voice rose. My blood pressure did, too. It even felt as though my hair was on fire. Could you drown in fire? I might be the first.

"An interesting thought to consider, isn't it?" I swear, the genie looked so smug he was this close to kissing his own ass. "Now, since you have reached a crossroads in all three wishes, your wishes are done."

"Wait! No! I'm not ready for this! Not for any of this!" My internal anger? Frustration? I wasn't sure what—rose.

"Well, it's here, whether you like it or not. So, according to our bargain, I shall take the time to deliberate, and then put you where it is I feel you will do best going forward."

"Are you sure that was our bargain? After all, it was three years ago, give or take a bit, and you might not remember."

The look he gave me could have cut steel. "Djinn do not forget. I get to choose your fate. It's my reward for the work I did to give you three wishes. Bargain's been made, Toots. You'll just have to wait and see."

"We also discussed that I could have a say in it."

"You have had your say. We've talked quite a bit; extensively after the first two do-overs. I've had the time to watch you in this last one, it being so long. My suggestion is to get some rest, and we'll settle this in the morning."

With a slight puff, he was gone. The bastard. He always poofed out of here when the questions got intense. I was ready to kill him.

I had to do this. It had been three years, but I had to do this. I looked down. I was still in in the clothes from my wine-drinking session. I got up, and went to my laptop. When I checked the date, it was the day after I'd met Dhameer. How does he do that, all the backing and forthing with time? Trying to figure it out made my head hurt. I gave up. The time thing—Dhameer handled that, and I wasn't going to get into it. Other than I'd just spent the three most amazing years in a wish. Where all my wishes had collided. What the hell?

I took a shower, and then checked my email. Nothing of major import, other than notes from X. I glanced at them, trying to remember what it was I did in this life.

It was weird. In both this and the third wish, I worked for him. He wanted me to, trusted me to, and we kept our friendship. He had someone totally different doing his IT and web based work–some place down in Kentucky. G.A. Pepper & Associates. Funny how I remembered that because I'd had them vetted before I agreed to send a contract to them. I'd been so good at IT, and now, I felt like I'd have to learn it all over again. I wondered if G.A. Pepper might be hiring. Did they even exist in this world? That led me to trying to figure out the time thing, and the only place that led was a massive headache. I stopped trying to figure it all out. For now, at least.

The thought of starting over was so lowering that I closed the laptop and crawled into bed. How could I go back to this life? I remembered making big promises to change my life if this was the one Dhameer chose, but right now, actually looking down the barrel of needing to do that, I was tired. I didn't want to do anything, and I wanted my old life back. But which old life? I didn't know anymore. Not when all three were in the same room mere hours ago, all looking at me.

I couldn't solve this tonight—hell, I couldn't solve this at all. It was all in the hands of an overly smug genie. I pulled the covers up over my head and hoped for sleep. Maybe something would look different in the morning.

Dhameer

Where to put Tibby? He laughed to himself. There had never been any question. Once he'd removed her from her third wish, he knew where she needed to be. He wanted to hear what she had to say, and more importantly, what she thought. He hovered nearby as she slept, wanting to make sure that he had read the signs and made the right decision. The look on her face when she realized what Seth had said— priceless. That would go down as one of his favorite moments.

He thought about the three men who had helped to shape Tibby's wishes. She had a habit of allowing men to be part of her life. So be it. Some people were like that with the opposite sex. Tibby drew them in. It was natural that she would have them as a large part of her life.

She'd accepted that, finally. He planned to let her keep all her memories after he put here where she'd be for good. She'd learned a great deal. Moving forward, that knowledge would help her.

He almost felt like rubbing his hands in glee. He glanced up at the dark sky. Would morning never come? He couldn't wait to put the conclusion in motion.

Tibby

When I woke, I didn't want to. Didn't want to open my eyes, look around, get up, nothing. I wasn't given a choice.

"C'mon Tootsie Pop. It's time. Aren't you ready to get to your final destination?"

"That was a bad series of movies. No. Not when you say it like that."

Dhameer laughed loudly. He was far too fucking cheerful this morning. I glared at him, parrot-perching on my furniture again, and absolutely delighted with himself.

"Let's get this done so I can start dealing with whatever needs to be dealt with."

"So optimistic, are you?"

I didn't want to tell him I was very afraid I'd open my eyes and be right here, in this dinky apartment, still lying in bed. So instead, I crossed my arms and glared at a spot on the wall.

"You're not really a morning person. That's all right. Close your eyes, Tabitha. Let's go home, shall we?"

***

When I felt myself shift and then settle, I didn't move. I was afraid to open my eyes. Afraid to see where I was. How long I sat there, I couldn't tell. Finally, slowly, ever so slowly, I opened my eyes.

I was in my car. In my Thing. In the parking lot of O'Hare's Bar.

I whooped, my heart pounding so madly I thought it was going to jump out of my chest. I started to cry. This was where I wanted to be. This was my life. This was where I was meant to be, and I was so thrilled and thankful Dhameer had seen it.

"Dhameer!" I yelled. I didn't care that people walking by might think I was insane. "Come and sit with me! I want to talk to you!"

He poofed into my car, and for the first time, I didn't care about the glitter.

"Why did you choose here?"

"Isn't this where you are supposed to be?"

I smiled at him, warm and happy. "Yes."

"You still have things that need to be attended to, Toots. You need to settle things with Rick and Seth. Your partner, no doubt, will have questions and will need to be told something."

I gripped his arm. I think he glared, but I wasn't paying attention. "Can I tell Bryant? And X?"

"You may tell whomever you like. I caution you, though, to think of what the recipients of your tale will think."

"Can I talk to Rick about it?"

"You may indeed."

"Can I talk to Seth about it?" Somewhere, I knew my questions were tedious, but again, didn't care. I wanted this to be very specific, with no catches.

"Absolutely."

I took his hand in both of mine. Turned to him, in the car. "Thank you. Before, I would have been a mess, even more than I am now, about what to do with these two men from my past. I would have thrown away my life with Bryant and my work for one of them, or both. Now, I have a life that I built for me. By myself. Which means, if one of these guys is right for me, I'm ready for it."

He smiled. It was such a big, warm smile that I was reminded of Seth. "You've got it in one, Tabitha. Do you know which one it will be?"

"I think so. But I'm not the only deciding factor here."

"With that, it's time for me to go."

"Wait! Will I see you again?"

"Probably not. After all, what in the world could you wish for now? I'll look in on you, Toots. It's always nice to see my success stories." Then he was gone.

I felt the tears start down my face. I didn't realize that he would be one of the things I missed once this whole wish thing was over. It had been such a big part of my life for a number of years, I felt Dhameer was a constant.

Except he wasn't. I wiped my eyes. I would just have to make him proud, and be one of his success stories. I started the car and headed to my boat. I didn't have the strength to face Bryant right now.

Once I made it back to the boat, I changed and curled up on my settee. I didn't want to do anything but cocoon tonight. Just as I'd gotten snuggled in, my cell rang.

I was watching TV, and I answered it absently. "Hello?"

"Tibby? It's Rick." His voice was deep, and I could tell he was in the middle of some strong emotion. It was so weird—I *knew*. Because I'd spent a year being as close with him as possible.

"Hi, Rick. I thought we were meeting tomorrow?"

"I couldn't stop thinking about you, and I don't want to wait to talk to you until tomorrow. Can we meet tonight?"

My heart fluttered in anticipation. This was my Rick. Open, forthright, didn't play games. I smiled into the phone. "I'm kind of settled in for the night, but if you don't mind casual, you're welcome to come over."

I gave him the address and slip number for the marina, and then ran to the head. I needed to look decent, even if I was going casual. Within the hour, I heard someone walking up the dock, and then there was a soft knock on the hull.

I stuck my head out. Rick stood next to the boat, hands in his pockets. He looked…distraught. Like tonight had already been a long night for him.

"Come on in."

He stepped carefully onto the deck and made his way down into the salon.

"Have a seat. Can I get you a drink?"

"No, I don't think so. Well, maybe some water." He sat while I got a bottle from the fridge, filled a glass with ice, and gave it to him.

"So what brings you here?"

"You," he said simply. "I've never forgotten you, and then to see you across the table at work, really shocked me."

I smiled. "That makes two of us. What did you think, after things returned to normal?"

He cocked his head at me, not understanding the question. "I don't know what you mean. When were things not normal?"

I opened my mouth, and then closed it. "Remind me of the last time we saw each other—it's been a long day, and I'm a little fuzzy." I pasted a smile on my face to hide the growing sick feeling in my stomach.

He leaned back, obviously more comfortable now that I asked something he could answer. "I think at graduation. You came to see me and Jake at graduation, remember?"

"Mostly you," I said quietly, and he smiled. "I do remember. That's right. You both went on a road trip that summer, didn't you?"

He nodded. "What did you do afterwards, Tib? I always wondered."

"I got a scholarship to Tech, and then went to DC for law school," I couldn't look at him. He didn't remember. He didn't remember! Why? Why would Dhameer tell me I could talk to him if he didn't remember? It had been years, and the loss of being the only one to remember made my heart break all over again.

"That's pretty impressive. Are you married?" He asked that last one hesitantly.

"No, haven't found the right one." I smiled at him sadly. "You?"

"Oh, yeah. Wife and two kids. They're at her parents' right now." He leaned forward to pull out a wallet, and show me their pictures. She was beautiful, although I noted she looked a bit like me.

He looked up from the picture to me. "She reminded me of you when I met her."

My heart cracked so loudly I was surprised he couldn't hear it. I pasted a smile on my face.

"She's lovely, Rick. So are your children. Thank you for showing them to me. I'm sure you're a wonderful father." I don't know how I kept my voice steady. I'd thought about kids with Rick. Now he had them with someone else.

He smiled, unaware of anything amiss. "Thanks. They're great. I'd love to have you and Bryant over for dinner, once we sort through this. I did a little reading when I got back to the office. You two are highly respected in the field. And you're working with XTC, as well? Didn't he live in the neighborhood?"

I was tired. This was not what I'd expected. Not even close. I didn't have the strength for this small talk. Why had he come here if this was his intention? Why couldn't this wait until tomorrow? "Yes, he did. We're still good friends."

"That must be exciting!" He laughed. Then he stood. "I appreciate you letting me barge in. I wanted to clear up any misunderstanding caused by my outburst this afternoon. I'm not usually so unprofessional. I didn't realize you knew Seth, as well. He's a great guy. But now that we've talked a bit, it's all good, yes?"

I nodded. He smiled, and headed out and off my boat. I felt the boat rock as he stepped onto the dock, unaware of the devastation he left behind him.

He didn't remember. He didn't know what had happened. He'd never know. He'd found a great wife and had two great kids.

The weight of all that I lost from that first wish flattened me. I lay on the settee and cried until long after midnight.

***

The next morning, I woke when my cell phone rang.

"H'llo?"

"Tib, are you coming into work today? It's after eight!" Bryant's disapproval rang through my head. I felt like I'd been out all night partying.

"Bryant, I think I'm coming down with something. I need to take the day off."

"Did you stay on the *Hyacinth*?"

"I did."

"Did you see Seth McKay last night?"

"I did."

"And?"

"It was hard. We had some history, some of it…challenging."

"Oh. This is something you haven't shared with me, Tib. Now I'm dying to know. But I'll table my vulgar need to know to be your friend and ask you if you're okay?"

"No, I'm not. I need a day or two. Can you cover for me? Then I'll tell you everything."

"Okay. I ought to warn you, though."

"About?"

"Seth McKay already stopped by, huge bouquet of roses in hand. Rather put out that you weren't here. I might have mentioned something about a boat." Bryant almost sounded apologetic.

"Why would you do that?" Now I was mad.

"Because whatever it is, you need to face it. First, because you do, and second, because we're going to see more of them through work. Funny as that meeting yesterday was, it can't be like that again."

"Message received, loud and clear, Captain."

"Good," he said, obscenely cheerful. "Deal with it, and then take notes. I want all the sordid details."

"Bye, Bryant."

"Love you! Bye!"

I ended the call and tossed the phone onto the settee next to me. Shit. Fuck. Hell. This was not how I pictured things going.

How did I picture them? If I was honest, I figured that Rick would remember, and it would be poignant, and touching, and I would finally get to

229

choose. To make the choice I hadn't been able to make—Rick or Seth. But Rick didn't remember. The thought of being forgotten, hell, not even being known, of there not being any awareness, saddened me. It felt like someone had…died.

I needed to be honest though. Would I choose Rick?

I had to think on that, for a long time. I had a lot of guilt over jumping from Rick to Seth. Apparently, that hadn't been necessary. He didn't even remember, and in fact, took what I started in him and built a life with someone else. That fact alone really hurt.

But would I have chosen him? I wasn't sure.

I didn't want to admit it. I'd been so committed to the idea of my first love. But I was forced to admit that I had to say no. Rick would not have been my choice, if I'd been given the choice. I wasn't one hundred percent sure, but I felt comfortable that it was at least in the nineties. Why? Why did I feel this way? Because he didn't remember? Because it made it easier to accept that I was the only person, other than Dhameer, who knew about that year we spent together?

I thought it over some more. That wasn't it, although there were definitely some sour grapes involved. It was, because, if given the choice, I had to look at how I felt with both of these men. It was a risk versus safety thing. Rick was safe. I knew that after the first wish, and I knew it now. I felt safe with him, and loved him for that. He'd given me safety when I felt I had none.

But Seth? Seth, as I'd noted before, had lots of risk involved. He represented the unknown, and

the scary, as far as my feelings were concerned. I
thought it about it some more.

He made me feel…incredible. Alive. Like I
could do anything. I knew after the second wish had
Dhameer left me there, I'd have fallen madly in love
with him. I'd been well on my way.

I'd thought I'd gone over this to the point of
insanity after the second wish, and settled how I felt.
But seeing them together today, having both of them
right in front of me at the same time threw all my
previous assumptions and navel gazing right out the
damn window.

I burst into tears.

I finally managed to get the tears to stop, and
went to the head to see how bad the damage was. I
looked dreadful. I gave up on fixing it and went and
dug into the fridge for something to eat. I hadn't been
on the boat in a while, so the pickings were scarce.
Thankfully, I always had cheese. I found some
crackers, and of course, there was a split of wine. So
with cheese and wine, I started to patch myself up.

My peace didn't last long. There was a
banging on the hull. I got up and popped my head
out of the hatch.

"I can hear you just fine at half the volume," I
said. I knew I was grumpy sounding, but I didn't care.
Not today.

"Good. I'd hate for you to miss my visit." It
was Seth.

Great. I looked like shit. My eyes were red and
puffy from crying. "Well. What do you want?" Is that
really what I wanted to say to him?

"I want to talk to you."

'Fine. Come aboard." I turned and went down the steps. Got another glass and poured the rest of the split for him. When he came down below, he looked around. "This is nice."

"Thank you. Wine?"

"Definitely."

We each drank for a moment. I took the bull by the horns.

"What do you know?"

He set down his wine glass. "I know everything." The look on his face was full of longing, of desire, and maybe even of love. Maybe I hadn't been alone in the falling in love bit.

It was too much. I burst into tears again, as though I hadn't cried enough today and put my head down on the table.

Seth got up instantly and sat next to me. "That's how I knew how you tasted after drinking my whiskey," he whispered into my ear. He rubbed my shoulders, and he was holding me to him, kissing my hair, and my forehead. As before, I felt safe and alive in his arms. No matter what lay ahead.

"You know what I really want?"

"What?"

"To know what happened to that little pink number you were wearing the last time I saw you? If I recall, you left at a most inopportune time, Tabitha."

I laughed. "I was so mad he yanked me then."

"That makes everyone."

"Everyone who?"

"Who was ready to kill Dhameer?" He lifted my chin up. "But we've found our way back, Tibby. I'll buy you all the pink nighties you want to wear. Just don't make me wait any longer."

Oh glory and hallelujah! I stood up, and stripped off my clothes so fast that he didn't even have time to blink before I was naked. I put my hands on my hips. "Well?"

"Well, what?" He seemed stunned by my supersonic loss of clothing.

"You going to make me be naked all by myself?"

He laughed, a loud, joyful laugh. Then he smiled, and it was the megawatt smile I remembered. And loved.

I took him, now appropriately undressed, into my arms. Snuggled up to those abs and that man that made everything better. "I love you," I said.

"I've always loved you."

He bent his head to my neck, and kissed me along the line of my jaw. My head tipped back, loving the feel of this man touching me. I'd never felt this light, this free, when being sexual with anyone. Not in any of my wishes, not in my initial run on life. Not, I thought with a pang, even with Rick. In the midst of all my realizations, and growing self-awareness, I'd almost missed the right thing for me right in front of me. True love was free, forgiving, accepting. It allowed for that in all—

"Hey." His voice broke into my thoughts.

"What?"

"Stop thinking. It's sex time."

Oh my.

With those words, he picked me up. "Where on this infernal sardine can is the bed?"

I pointed towards the bow, and he moved in that direction immediately. For a boat, I've got a pretty swanky bed set up. Seth tossed me into my cushy bed without a second thought and was on top of me before I'd caught my breath.

"I've thought of you every day for years," he whispered into my ear as his hands moved down my body. He cupped them under my ass, and I felt my entire body go up in flames.

"I've missed you. I've cursed that damn genie to hell and back, and he doesn't even have the courtesy to answer. But now," he took my nipple into his mouth. "Now, I can forgive him. He brought you back to me."

He moved up to kiss me. "I don't think I can wait all that long. I can't be all lovey dovey. I've seen you in my head every day for the past three years, beckoning to me in that nightie." He devoured my mouth.

I couldn't get a word in. I found that I didn't want to. I wanted to touch him, feel him, get so close to him that I felt I could crawl inside him.

"Then let's not wait this time. We've got plenty of time afterwards."

"I didn't bring anything."

"What? What kind of sailor are you? I am always prepared." I reached into a small drawer at the side of my bed and handed him the small packet. He looked like he wanted to say something but I shook it in his face. "Time's a-wasting, sport!"

He grabbed it, tore it open, and rolled it on. He looked as good naked as I remembered. Better.

Then he was on top of me again, and between my legs. In an instant, we were one. It was the most amazing thing I'd ever known.

He looked me in the eye, and even as we both got closer and closer, he never broke his gaze. When I cried out, he covered my mouth with his. A moment later, he groaned and dropped his head to my neck.

I didn't want to move. I didn't want him to move. We didn't leave my boat for three days.

EPILOGUE

Granddad looked around the small group assembled on the deck. He smiled at me as we listened to Seth make his vows in a strong voice. Then I saw him looking with a hint of disapproval at X. Tough shit, old man. My best friend. I glared at him. For once, X was going solo. It was a good look on him.

Next to X was Bryant. Only I would have a wedding party that consisted of mostly men. But these were the friends who had been with me since we'd met, and I was lucky to have them. In honor of my color choice, both wore the saucy pink ties and waistcoats that matched my flowers. Next to Bryant stood Danni. Will was Seth's best man, and she and I had rekindled our friendship. That meant almost as much as finding Seth again.

Someone cleared their throat. Oh. Apparently I was navel gazing. I gave an apologetic smile to Granddad. He lowered his brows and made another old man kind of noise in the back of his throat.

Granddad turned to Seth. "You got the ring?"
Seth pulled it from his pocket.
"Well then, let's get it on her finger."
He turned to me and held it out, an offering. A choice.

I put my hand up, and he slid it on.

"By the power probably mistakenly vested in me by the District of Columbia, I now pronounce you man and wife," Granddad boomed. "You may now salute your bride!"

Seth reached a hand out to me, placing it gently on my cheek. He drew me in, caressing the line of my face.

"You're all I've ever wished for, Tabitha McKay."

"You're my wish come true."

His lips came down on mine. I could swear I saw a flash, but when Seth finally let me go, I gazed up at the sky, and I couldn't see a thing.

Then I met Seth's eyes and looked into my future.

Dhameer

If djinn were actually given to tears or excessive emotion, he might feel the need to cry. It was the only time he'd ever seen a paired set of wishes end up like this. Oh, there had been wishes that spurred others, but never a paired set of them. Not like this. And for the pair to end up together? *There ought to be a Hall of Fame*, he thought. *I'd be a first draft pick for it.*

Something caught his attention below. It wasn't Tibby or her groom. No, they were beyond him now. They had made the path they needed for their future.

He swirled down for a closer look. In the bright sun of the day, he was just another ray.

"Ah. There you are." He smiled. "I still got it." He drew in a deep breath, and then sent out of a puff of air that glittered down into the small group on the boat.

On the deck, Xavier, also known as XTC, badass rapper, shook his head. Where had that dust come from? He rubbed his hand over his face and head. He looked up. There was nothing in the sky. So what had just fallen on him?

"X, come on!" Tibby called him. "Cake!"

Still rubbing his head, Xavier followed her. He'd have to make sure to scrub down before getting into bed tonight. No telling what germs he might pick up.

Three Wishes

Lisa Manifold

ABOUT THE AUTHOR

Lisa Manifold lives in the amazing state of Colorado with her husband, two Darling Boys, two dogs, and a perpetually offended cat. She is an avid reader, skier, and costumer. You can find her online at:

www.lisamanifold.com

Book 2 of the Heart of the Djinn series is coming soon.
Follow Xavier's story in
FORGOTTEN WISHES